WARSAW COMMUNITY HIGH SCHOOL
1 Tiger Lane
Warsaw IN 46580

JUMPING OFF TO FREEDOM

Anilú Bernardo

PIÑATA BOOKS
HOUSTON, TEXAS
1996

This volume is made possible through grants from the National Endowment for the Arts (a federal agency) and the Andrew W. Mellon Foundation.

Piñata Books are full of surprises!

Piñata Books
A Division of Arte Público Press
University of Houston
452 Cullen Performance Hall
Houston, Texas 77204-2004

Cover art and design by Gladys Ramirez

Bernardo, Anilú,
    Jumping off to freedom / by Anilú Bernardo.
      p.   cm.
    Summary: Courage and desperation lead fifteen-year-old David and his father to flee Cuba's repressive regime and seek freedom by taking to the sea on a raft headed for Miami.
    ISBN 1-55885-088-0 (paper : alk. paper)
    1. Cubans—Florida—Juvenile fiction. [1. Cubans—Florida—Fiction. 2. Refugees—Fiction.] I. Title.
PZ7.B455137Ju   1996
[Fic]—dc20   95-37667
                                             CIP
                                              AC

2 3 4 5 6 7 8 9 10   10 9 8 7 6 5 4 3

Special thanks to Jim, my husband and best friend, who has always believed in me.

Thank you Nancy Cohen and Cindy Thomason for keeping me on track.

To my daughters Stephanie and Amanda. May they one day touch the beauty of Cuba, my land of birth.

In memory of the many Cubans who have lost their lives in the quest for freedom.

With heartfelt gratitude to Brothers to the Rescue pilots Mario de la Peña and Carlos Costa for their help in researching this story. They, together with Armando Alejandre and Pablo Morales, were shot and killed in 1996 as they flew in search of Cuban rafters to rescue.

JUMPING OFF TO FREEDOM

Chapter

1

"Why are you taking me away?" The desperate young man yelled. He struggled helplessly against the two armed and uniformed State Security guards. "I haven't done anything wrong!"

David's menacing fists were quickly restrained behind him in tight handcuffs. His unbuttoned plaid shirt flew open, exposing tiny streams of sweat that ran over his young muscular chest. He swung his head and shoulders from side to side, like an ox, powerless against a restraining yoke. David's attempts to shake his captors aside were in vain.

"Where are you taking me? I haven't done anything!" David shouted angrily.

Without a word, the two men in green uniforms escorted him to their Russian-made jeep.

A crowd had gathered. Those in front were morbidly pleased at the break in the boring afternoon. Others, cautiously peeking through the gaps in the crowd, feared they were watching another unjustified trip to prison. It didn't take much to be picked up and investigated. A groundless suspicion by the neighborhood committee or a neighbor's envy were enough to earn a report and a swift trip to the local detention center. In Cuba's socialist system, the accused was guilty unless he could convince the government of his innocence.

The military guards shoved David to the back of the jeep, and as they slammed the door shut, Elena turned and ran away in tears.

~~~~~~

"*Señora* Leal! Open the door! Quickly!" Elena shouted through the open window. She banged the door with her fists, repeating her urgent cries. She had covered the two blocks at a fast sprint and now had no recollection of the run. She could think only of David's look of helpless terror as he was shoved into the jeep.

Rosa Leal, her short dark hair neatly combed, stepped out to the porch. Her husband Miguel hurried to the door, barefooted.

"What's wrong, Elena?"

Rosa wanted to continue the questioning, but the girl's horror spilled out in a torrent of sobs. Rosa pulled the fourteen-year-old to her. She liked Elena, David's girlfriend. Rosa suspected the sweethearts had quarreled.

Elena wrenched herself free from the protective embrace. "He's been taken away! David's been arrested!" she cried out.

Rosa froze.

"What are you saying, girl?" Miguel Leal leaned forward and roughly jerked Elena's arm.

"They took him! They drove him away!" the girl said between sobs.

Their son was in serious trouble. David had never given his parents worry.

"He tried to fight them off. He struggled. But they handcuffed him and pushed him into the jeep." Elena's words came out of her mouth like machine-gun bullets, swift and deadly.

"He shouldn't have resisted. That makes things even worse!" Rosa moaned with worry.

"Why did they arrest him?" Miguel asked. His dark eyebrows knitted in anger.

"They kept asking him about his bicycle. Where was it? What did he do with it?" Elena's voice was high and strained, tears running down her reddened cheeks. "He told them he had lent it to Pepe Alonso."

"Yes, David told us Pepe wanted to borrow it." Recovering from the shock of the news, Rosa stepped between her husband and the shaken girl. "Don't you remember, Miguel? It was three nights ago."

He released his grip on the girl's arm. "I knew that wasn't a good idea. Pepe is always taking risks. He shouldn't have involved my fifteen-year-old in his shady dealings." Miguel's fist landed on his open palm, the only acceptable release to his anger.

"There was nothing we could do about it." Rosa's eyes welled with tears. "David had already loaned it to him."

"David should know better. We didn't come by the bike that easily." Miguel shook his head in frustration.

The family's two bicycles were their only means of transportation. With Cuba's gasoline supply and automobile parts from Russia cut off and public vehicles in disrepair, the country relied on its fleet of Chinese bicycles. Not everyone could afford one. The family had sacrificed to buy a used one for David, which he rode to school and for family errands.

"I know, Miguel. But we've also taught him to lend a hand to friends."

"Well, that's one friend that's in trouble. You can be sure Pepe used the bicycle for some black-market deal and now they've got him, too." Tucking in his shirt, Miguel asked Elena, "Where did they take him?"

The girl shook her head and raised up her palms. New tears streamed down her cheeks.

David counted thirty-five push ups. There was little else he could do in the cramped cell he shared with two others for the last three days. They took turns exercising and stretching, though each session lasted a short time. The men were weak from the small rations. There were only small slits in the wall for ventilation in the stuffy cell, which was made worse with summer heat.

David had heard that this was a holding facility. Detainees were kept here while their investigation was in progress. If found guilty, the prisoners were then moved to a long-term prison.

Every day, David was taken out for interrogation. Every day, he denied any wrongdoing. The questioning lasted several hours. They told David little about the evidence against him. He hoped this meant the authorities didn't have much to go on. He had not been beaten, probably because of his young age. But the fear of being roughed up loomed over David's head and helped him control his temper.

He and his cellmates knew beating prisoners was common, so when the cell door was opened, they all shuddered.

"David Leal. Come with me," a young thin guard called out.

Another interrogation, David figured. His cell mates looked away, unwilling to meet his fearful eyes.

Rosa and Miguel Leal sat in stiff wooden chairs in the waiting area of the local detention center. Over the objections of the guards, they had spent the night sitting in this hallway. It was nearly ten in the morning when the clatter of footsteps on the tile floor announced David's entrance, followed by his unsmiling escort.

"¡*Mi hijo!*" Rosa ran and embraced her tired son.

Though glad to see his parents, David's shoulders stiffened. "I'm all right, Mami."

Miguel put a hand on David's shoulder and nodded. They would have time to talk later, away from the presence of the hated men in uniform.

"Come and sign this paper!" The young guard directed David to a desk, where a much older sergeant sat and smoked a cigar. The man looked relaxed and sure of his job.

"I'm not signing any confession!" David said through clenched teeth, boldly meeting the man's eyes. "I told you I'm not guilty of anything!"

The guard grinned, enjoying David's indignation. "This is a release form. If you don't sign it, you can't go," he said slowly, his voice heavy with sarcasm. Then, he cocked his head and shrugged. "You decide."

Defiantly, David grabbed the form from the taunting man's hand. "Let me read it."

"I'll read it with you," said Miguel, barely controlling his anger. "I don't want them to pull any tricks on you."

The sergeant released a puff of pungent smoke. Closely inspecting his cigar, as though the drama in front of him were of little importance, he said, "We don't work that way."

⚓⚓⚓⚓⚓⚓

"Did they hurt you, *mi hijo*?" Rosa asked as soon as the family walked out into the sunlight.

Rosa was always concerned for him. He dismissed her fussing with a shrug. "No they didn't rough me up. They just questioned me for hours."

"What were they holding you for, *hijo*?" Miguel tried to rub the tension from his temple.

"They caught Pepe Alonso in a pasture by the fresh carcass of a cow. They say he killed the cow and it was government property..."

"There is no other kind of cattle in this country, David," his father corrected. "Every goat, pig and cow is numbered and accounted for."

"They thought I took part in it because my bicycle was abandoned nearby with a bundle of beef tied to the back. I told them I had nothing to do with the butchering, that I had only lent him the bicycle. Then, they insisted I was to be paid with beef for the use of the bicycle." He shook his head in disbelief, as though the whole affair had been a bad dream.

David's dark hair was matted and dull from days of neglect. Rosa examined her son as they walked. Though he had reached the size of a grown man, his clear green eyes still held the hope of youth. "Lord knows, we could have used the meat." She sighed. "I haven't been able to give the family a decent meal in weeks."

"But Mami, how could I have given you the meat?" He raised his hands in exasperation. How could his mother doubt him? "I had nothing to do with stealing it."

"I know that, *mi hijo*. I was just thinking aloud," Rosa said softly.

"That's what makes me so mad," David continued venting his frustration. "They had no proof. The bicycle could have been stolen from me. No matter how I denied it, they kept telling me I should admit to the conspiracy and to destroying and stealing government property."

"David, this government will always assume the worst in a situation. It's up to the accused to clear himself. Just remember that," his father said somberly, disdain etched in his eyes.

"Over and over they said I was dealing on the black market with Pepe. They asked me where I had been on Tuesday night." David was still furious. It was hard to take such treatment when you were clearly innocent.

"I certainly hope you are not putting yourself in such dangerous situations." Rosa eyed her son with concern.

His mother persisted in questioning his involvement. He exploded, "I simply lent him my bicycle! It was only fair. Pepe has done many favors for us before. Where do think we get our fresh vegetables?"

Miguel gave his son a quick meaningful look. "David, your mother has been through a lot. Don't raise your voice to her. She's only looking out for you." He glanced around, but no one was within hearing. "Besides, some things are better left unsaid. You never know who can hear you."

They were approaching the public transit stop. These days, cattle trucks, with benches along the sides, served as buses, as there were few buses still in working order. Personal automobiles were a far off-dream from another time. The thirty-year-old models, which still roamed the otherwise motor-free streets, were used as taxis to cart tourists to beaches and restaurants reserved for foreigners. The family had no choice but to wait for the next public transport vehicle.

"*Mi hijo*, we've been so worried for you." Rosa glanced at his sweaty shirt and dirty gray pants. "They wouldn't tell us anything. Your father tried to speak to the commandant and tell him you were a minor."

"Those brazen thugs just kept brushing me off." Miguel shook his head, re-living his frustration with the military, whom he considered shameless. "On the first two days, your mother and I went to headquarters to plead your case. They wouldn't even discuss the charges against you. I bet I could have gotten you out in no time if I'd greased their filthy palms with some American dollars." He shook his head regretfully. "I just didn't have any."

"You would have landed in the same cell, Miguel," Rosa said without hesitation. "You know common citizens are not allowed to handle dollars."

"It's the only currency of value in the streets these days." Miguel's bottom lip jutted out in a dissatisfied pout. Dollars could be had only when sent from a relative in the United States or when selling something to foreign tourists.

Miguel continued recounting their fruitless attempts to free David. "Yesterday, we refused to leave until we could see you."

"We stayed here all night," Rosa said with a nod, affirming their loyalty to their son. "I guess your father's stubborn demands finally paid off."

Miguel shrugged. "They simply had nothing solid to hold against him." The tall muscular man turned to his son. "This morning, they said the investigation was over and you could go home."

David's lips pursed with irritation. "Without my bicycle! They are keeping that for evidence against Pepe."

"I bet we'll see that bicycle on the streets in a few weeks." Miguel drew his green eyes into a menacing squint. "One of those guards will pad his wallet selling it for a few bucks."

They stood apart from the waiting crowd and kept their voices low.

"Any news on Pepe's fate? I didn't see him there," David asked apprehensively.

"Word on the street is that they caught him in the act. He was cornered like a penned wolf, standing over the butchered cow. He had no chance to run away, but his partner was able to escape."

"Who was the man who ran off on him? We should teach him a lesson!" David said, his hands coiling into tight fists.

"I don't want you in anymore trouble!" Rosa admonished, raising her eyes to the heavens.

"His name is Tomás Pico. Pepe's friends are angry at him for leaving Pepe stranded. I doubt that anyone will inform on Pico, though. You know how we keep a code of silence against the police."

"Because of that traitor, I spent three nights in that stinking jail!" David said angrily.

"But now you're back with us," Miguel said to appease him. "It's over for you. Pepe is the one I feel sorry for."

"And he's only eighteen," Rosa moaned.

"His crime is taken more seriously than murder," David added. His cell mates had told him about others sharing the same fate. "Killing a cow is considered destroying government property. His penalty will easily be seven or eight years in prison."

"You can't take chances with these things, *hijo*." Miguel shook his head in frustration.

"So, what are we supposed to eat? We've got to do illegal things to survive!" David spat the words out angrily, his fists clenching tightly. "A pound of rice doesn't last us two days, and that's what the government sells us for a week."

"Leave the risks to your father. He's cautious." Rosa feared her son's eagerness and youth were a dangerous combination. "It's a man's job to figure out what to do for his family, anyhow."

David bit his lip to control his rage. His mother just couldn't accept that he could be cunning and street smart. "You well know each of us has to do his part to help out. You do your bartering, when you can."

After an uncomfortable silence, Rosa asked David, "Did you eat?"

"Bread in the morning, rice at night. Washed it down with water that runs from a pipe for only ten minutes a day."

"You didn't get the food I brought you? I traded with neighbors and brought you a hard boiled egg and bread everyday. The guard said he'd take them to you."

"That's good food gone to waste! I bet you the guard ate it as soon as he rounded the corner out of your sight." David dismissed the idea with a toss of his chin, pretending it was not a big deal. He didn't like his mother fussing over him. But the mention of food had started his mouth watering. "Look, there aren't many privileges there. I was in a cell maybe three meters by four meters with two other men. A drain served as our toilet. They took me out only for interrogation."

"Filthy scum!" Miguel yelled roughly.

"Miguel, you can say what you want when we get home," his wife cautioned anxiously. Negative words against the government could get a person reported. "There's too many ears within range."

"Where did you leave Diana?"

"Your sister is at your uncle's house. She is worried for you. We all were." Both Rosa and Miguel nodded.

David was quiet for a few minutes, looking for a way to ask his next question. He didn't want his parents to think he gave it much importance. "Have you heard from Elena?"

Rosa tried to hide the little smile that crept up to her lips. "She comes by everyday to find out the latest news about you."

"She came running to tell us about your arrest. She was frantic about her poor David." Miguel chuckled at his son's poorly concealed interest. "She saw all your fighting and struggling and told us how they had to shove you into the jeep."

David squared his shoulders with a new-found pride. "They said I was plenty guilty, and the proof was in my attitude. Those idiots claim that resisting arrest is a sign of guilt."

"That's no joking matter, *hijo*," Miguel said somberly. "You've got to control that temper of yours. It's only going to get you trouble."

"Maybe you should practice some of your own advice, my dear husband." Rosa laughed for the first time in days.

~~~~~~

"Don't think you can sweet-talk me with a present! After what you did to Pepe, I've lost my respect for you!" The girl tossed her long brown curls over her shoulder with disdain. She let Tomás into the living room and closed the door behind him.

"I didn't leave him stranded!" Tomás had repeated the story to her so many times, his voice was full of frustration. He really liked Mirta and wanted her to believe him. "Pepe and I had a system. I was to take the packaged meat to a hiding place while he continued butchering. I had just packed the bicycle when the police arrived. Only a fool would return to stand by Pepe's side!"

"At least that would have shown some loyalty to your friend. Instead you ran and hid."

Tomás' jaw dropped. "I ran and hid like anyone with sense would have done. They would have locked me up too. What good would I be to Pepe in jail?"

"What good are you to him now?" she asked, her hands on her hips.

"At least I was able to take some meat to his mother. I'm not the kind to benefit from a friend's misery." Tomás fanned his head with his hat. He ran his fingers through his dark hair to keep it from sticking out wildly on the sides.

"Is that what's in this package?" Mirta took the heavy bundle from him and brought it to her nose. She closed her eyes and sniffed deeply.

Tomás smiled. He was sure she had not enjoyed the smell of fresh beef in months. He wanted to take her in his arms and kiss her full on the mouth.

"Poor Pepe will not be served a decent meal for years," Mirta said. As she opened her eyes, he saw they were glazed with sadness. She pointed an accusatory finger at Tomás "They've also taken in that poor boy who loaned Pepe the bicycle. They think he's the one who helped Pepe butcher the cow."

A wave of shame warmed up Tomás' cheeks. Word was out that a boy named David Leal was under investigation. "What am I supposed to do? Turn myself in? They'll put me in prison for certain, but there's no guarantee they'll let go of the Leal boy."

Unable to answer his questions, Mirta shook her head with annoyance. "All I know is you deserted Pepe!"

"Why don't you ask Pepe himself? Get the story from him!" Tomás challenged her. He knew how difficult it was to visit a prisoner. But she could talk to Pepe, she would see Tomás wasn't lying. Then, Mirta would trust him again.

"I will. I can't wait to see him. As soon as I get permission I will run to his side." Mirta's dark eyes were teary and dreamy.

Tomás shook his head. Mirta had taken hold of Tomás' heart. But it appeared it was Pepe who ruled hers. Tomás grabbed her arms and pulled her to him. The heavy package pressed against his chest as she held it defensively between them.

"Don't you understand? It wasn't my fault he got caught!"

"Get your hands off me! Don't ever touch me again!" Mirta wrinkled her nose as though he smelled rotten. An icy stab pierced his heart. He couldn't accept that she no longer cared for him.

"Come on, Mirta," Tomás said with an unsure smile. "I thought you could cook a couple of steaks for us tonight."

"Not in a million years!"

Tomás let go of her angrily. "Look! If I had deserted him, Pepe would be mad at me. He would have turned me in as his partner. But the police don't know who I am!"

"Maybe it's time they did!" Mirta spun around and, holding the bundle of beef tightly to her breast, ushered him out the door.

Tomás walked out without a word, snorting angrily. He turned the ignition on the government truck assigned to him. Losing Mirta had left him miserable and lonely. She was convinced he had betrayed Pepe. Nothing seemed to change her mind. She was blinded by her new-found love for Pepe. He clenched his fists in frustration. If Mirta followed through on her threat and turned him in, he'd lose his best years rotting in a cell.

Perhaps it was time to be looking for a way out of the country.

Rosa rushed into the kitchen to fix her son a meal. She had hoarded and put aside staples in anticipation of his homecoming.

When the neighbors saw the family return with the freed young man, they crowded into the house. They were eager to welcome David and to hear him tell of his ordeal. Someone ran to alert Miguel's brother, Roberto, who lived a few blocks away. Few families had working telephones. A quick run was the fastest way to carry news.

Soon, twelve-year-old Diana had her arms around her older brother. She kept her hands on his shoulders, afraid to let go of him, as David wolfed down a plate of rice with red beans and sweet plantains. Rosa regretted that she didn't have any meat or fish to give her son. None had been available when she had gone to buy their monthly food allotment. To make up for it, Rosa piled David's plate high by cutting the rest of the family's portions.

David relished retelling his experiences to the mesmerized audience.

As the light grew dimmer and Miguel retold the group about his efforts to gain his son's release, David noticed a silent figure on the dark porch. He drank his ice water and, drawing little attention, stepped out the open door.

Elena shrank back shyly. "I'm so glad you're back," she said softly, delight washing over her clear face.

"I'm glad you came," he whispered, not wanting to be heard by the visitors. "I was thinking about you."

"Did they treat you badly?" Her fine eyebrows arched with uncertainty.

"Not too bad," he said valiantly. "But I had trouble sleeping on that hard concrete floor." He didn't have the courage to tell her that he had lain awake thinking of her.

"I couldn't sleep either. I had you on my mind the whole time. I was so worried." Soft brown curls caressed her gentle features and her eyes glistened with fresh moisture.

Jumping Off to Freedom

David took Elena's hand and led her to the private darkness under the mahogany tree. There, he kissed her soft trembling lips the way he had dreamed of doing during those long restless nights.

Chapter

2

 David was awakened by a raking, scraping noise outside his window. He bolted up in bed and listened. It was the sound of a heavy object being dragged over gravel. Burglars actively searched for anything that had value in the under-handed market of the streets. Though their home had never been hit, David was sure their turn had come up.

Wasting no time to pull on a pair of pants, he rushed into his parents' room.

"Papi! Papi! There's a burglar in the side yard!" he said in a hushed, urgent whisper.

A strange glow illuminated the room. The semi-darkness revealed unused pillows and bare sheets. He wondered where his parents could be in the middle of the night. Maybe they were investigating the noises.

Papi kept a wooden club under the bed—a safe weapon in case of threat within their home. David leaned under the mattress and gripped it tightly.

As he turned to leave the room, he was jolted by the dark outline of his mother in the corner. She faced the tiny flame of a small votive candle on the dresser at the foot of a ceramic statue of the Virgin of Charity, patroness of Cuba. Rosa's face was tilted up, her eyes were closed, her hands tightly clasped. Her prayerful concentration seemed to have taken her to a different dimension.

Since the days of his imprisonment, David had noticed a change in his parents. They argued over little details and hardly looked at each other. Mami had a detached, absorbed manner and, other than managing the daily chores, she hardly took part in family time. He had heard them fighting at night, in hushed tones behind closed doors. At times, Papi had left and spent the night at uncle Roberto's house. Perhaps that's where he had gone tonight, too.

"Where's Papi? There's a burglar outside." David was anxious to go. Hot blood raced in his veins.

Rosa's lips moved in silent prayer to the heavens. She was out of reach.

"I'm going out to get the dirty thief!" he snarled. "He's going to be one sorry lump when I get through with him!" David ran out of the bedroom. As he crossed the living room, he heard his mother's frantic voice.

"No! Don't go!"

He wouldn't let her stop him. He was strong and capable of much more than women could ever understand. With Papi gone, he'd have to cover the duties of the man of the house.

David darted out to the porch and bounded around the corner of the house. There, he crouched behind a clump of fish-tail palms to get a better feel for the direction of the noise. The dragging, rasping sound now came from further back in the pitch darkness of the yard.

"David, come back in!" his mother's alarmed whisper reached him. She would give him away, always worried for his safety.

David scuttled further into the darkness. He knew every plant and rock in his territory and skirted the obstacles expertly, as if he had a bat's natural sonar. His heart pounded in his chest.

David perceived the intruder's shadowy shape from the man's strained movements, as barely any light reflected from him. He had chosen an overcast night to carry out his thievery. Truly, the ruffian had no scruples.

The man had reached the concealing low branches of the large avocado. His loot, a long board which he pulled with much effort, now raked the brittle dead leaves on the ground.

David tightened his grip on the club. His breath was a fast pant. He crept ahead in a wide circle to intercept the man in his path. David stalked him carefully, aware a misstep on a crackling leaf would give him away. The prowler huffed with every drag of the heavy board.

Suddenly, David spurted forward, his club raised like a battle saber. "You'll pay for this! You low born scum!"

The man dropped the board and raised his hands in defense.

David charged through the avocado-laden branches. The hard pear-shaped fruit swung wildly as he raced through the overhanging tangle. A large avocado smacked David on the bridge of his nose. He lost his bearings momentarily and swung the club blindly.

The wooden bat met its mark. The man cursed in pain. David reached back for another violent down sweep. As swift as a lightning bolt, a strong hand grabbed the business end of the club and David's furious swing was stopped in mid air.

"Are you crazy?" His father barked in his face. "You are going to get us all killed!"

David was stunned. He had struck his own father. An icy feeling of shame reached his stomach. "I thought you were a burglar," he mumbled.

"Miguel, David, are you all right?" Rosa whispered anxiously at the edge of the low canopy.

"We're fine, Rosa. You'd better go back to the house, as we planned, in case a neighbor comes over to check on the noise," Miguel told his wife. "Pick up the other end of the board and help me," he commanded David with a harsh whisper.

They carried the heavy wood to the old garage. The doors to the wooden structure creaked from disuse. It had been years since it had housed a car, back at the time of David's grandfather. As a child, David had played with all the old junk stored in it and had hammered nails into its walls for practice.

"Just set it down easily," said Miguel. He lit an old kerosene lantern. The government had cut off electric service at night to conserve energy years earlier. It didn't matter. For his secret task, Miguel would not have chosen the bright glare of the electric fixture, anyway.

Miguel had piled up a number of boards about five meters long. Shorter planks of wood were stacked against the wall. Old canvas and coiled lengths of rope lay among the old junk in back. David knew something significant was taking place.

"*Hijo*." Miguel's serious tone stopped David's contemplation. "There are matters so threatening to a family's well being that parents don't dare to share them with their children." Miguel put his hands on his son's stone hard biceps. "By coming out here tonight, you have given me no option but to include you in my preparations. You're almost a man now. I can use your help."

David nodded his head solemnly. He would risk anything for his father.

Miguel rubbed his bruised shoulder where the club had struck. He took a pensive breath, then continued. "Your mother and I remember the old ways. Our families had plenty before communism took over our fertile homeland. I don't want you to live a life without opportunities, without rewards for your efforts." Miguel's steady gaze radiated calm. David listened intently.

"What I'm working on could land me in prison for years. Your poor mother would have to struggle alone to feed you and Diana." Miguel's eyes pierced his son's gravely. "I trust you will keep this to yourself."

"*Sí*, Papi. You can count on me. Always." David's voice was several octaves lower than usual. Though he appeared serene, excitement and apprehension twisted in his gut.

"We are sailing away to freedom," Miguel whispered as he watched his son's green eyes widen.

David's mouth opened in amazement. He drew in a deep breath and let it out slowly. "Are we building a boat?"

Miguel chuckled. "The best I can manage is a raft. There aren't enough parts to build an honest boat. But, it will have a sail and a rudder. We'll have a way to direct our destiny," he said, with a double dose of meaning.

"Are the four of us sailing off to the United States?" David asked eagerly.

Miguel couldn't look at him. "Your mother refuses to go. She wants Diana to stay with her."

"I don't want us all to die! It's a reckless crazy notion!" Rosa's distressed cry startled them. Soundlessly, she had entered the garage.

"Cuba is a prison, *hijo*!" Unsure of the power of Rosa's words on his son, Miguel pleaded with him. "Our homeland doesn't allow us choices. I can barely feed my family. A man is powerless to provide for his own."

"You'll be powerless in the vast ocean," Rosa countered, her tormented eyes searching her son's face for a sign of agreement.

Resisting her anguished fears, Miguel implored David, "In Cuba, there's a constant threat everywhere you go. A miscalculation lands you in jail. My very soul was captive while you were detained."

"And if I lose you both, will my soul rest?" Rosa's dark eyes pierced her son's. Her question needed no answer.

David looked from one to the other, watching the heavy ball of desperation bounce in this Ping-Pong match.

"Come September, you'll report to agrarian service." Miguel pointed a calloused finger at David's chest. His brows knitted gravely. "To earn a high school degree, you'll live in barracks in the countryside and work the fields. Your back will hurt. Your fingers will be raw from the labor. You'll be given the disgusting rations I was made to eat at your age, noodles carelessly stored so that weevils share your plate. After days of refusing the food, you become so weak that it begins to taste good, bugs and all."

"It wasn't that way for me. We had enough to eat." Her unsure voice died out.

"But there's nothing to eat now!" Miguel's tone rang with despair. "We are already feeding our children ground banana peels to stretch our rations! What do you think they'll feed him in the fields?"

Tears streaked down the anguished creases in Rosa's face. Moved by her pain, Miguel was gentle. "Rosa, you can't bear to see him taken away from us either, to have him labor for others under such conditions. If he's jailed again, if he can't control that temper of his, what will become of you?"

They were all silent. David mulled over every word he had heard. There was so much he wanted to do with his life. Yet, he hadn't dared dream. He felt restrained, fearful to make a move. Now, his father had opened a window into the future. And it was full of light, full of hope.

David placed his hands on Rosa's shoulders. "Mami, come with us," he asked earnestly and seared her heart with his decision.

Rosa's eyes welled with tears. Her tongue was silenced by agony. David had been swayed to take the risk. Her appeals had no use. She ran out of the old building.

"She needs some time alone. Let her go," Miguel said, seeing David hesitate. "We'll place an official request for them to join us when we arrive in the United States."

"Why don't we have your cousin Gabriel do that for us now? He lives in Miami." David's brows arched in hope.

"He can't, *hijo*. Only a parent, child or sibling can make a request for another to enter the United States. His blood ties to us are not sufficient."

Miguel propped up the new board against the stack of wood, indicating with his action that the raft was the only way of escape.

David lent him a hand. His neck prickled with excitement. "When will we start building it?"

"I'm waiting for a large block of packing foam that was used to ship equipment. Luis Fuentes works at the docks and he is saving the material for us. We're looking for a way to bring it here."

"Are you paying for it?"

"Of course! No one looks out for his neighbor these days, David."

"I suppose by paying him, you are also buying his silence."

Miguel looked up at his son, proud that the boy understood. "We are going to plan this out very carefully," he said, happy to finally take him into his confidence. "We'll have to put the raft in at the rocky cove. We can't take it to a beach too far away without a way to transport it. I've been studying the tides and the currents and as the time gets closer, we'll keep an eye on weather reports."

"I can do some fishing from the rocks to study the schedules and maneuvers of the Border Guard. I've seen their motor launches pass by the mouth of the cove in the evening."

"Excellent idea!" Miguel smiled at him, impressed by his plan.

"We'll make it, Papi." David offered his hand, sealing a man's pact. "We'll work together at this."

Several days later, David accompanied his father to a run-down warehouse in the waterfront district. Luis would meet them there once the place was deserted for the night. Instead of getting rid of the foamy packing material as his work supervisor had ordered, Luis had hidden it. The men planned to transfer the white block under the cover of darkness.

"What did I tell you?" Luis asked pointing to the white rectangle. The man was lean and sun-baked. "It is solid and dense. Just the right stuff to keep you afloat."

David and Miguel pounded on the block with their fists. There was no sign of giving. David lifted a corner of the block and it came off the floor effortlessly.

Miguel scratched his head, unwilling to appear too eager. He walked around the foam block as David held it up. There was no sign of cracks or other damage. It was just what he wanted.

"I've got the two hundred pesos." Miguel tipped his head, agreeing to the deal.

David winced. Two hundred pesos was a man's wages for a month. It was all one could expect to earn legally and yet not enough to feed a family. A chicken on the black market could easily fetch thirty pesos. Ten pounds of root vegetables, a necessary staple in every home, could be had for no less than fifty pesos. That's if a man was cunning enough to find a dealer with a ready supply.

Most dealers preferred to be paid with dollars. The Leal family was struggling. Miguel's cousin Gabriel worked in a factory in Miami. His wages were grand by the standards of his Cuban relatives, but they knew his was a modest life. From time to time, he sent U.S. dollars to his parents and in-laws. Once, Gabriel's mother gave a pair of leather shoes to Rosa. He had sent her the wrong size. Rosa treasured them. Usually, though, there wasn't much to spare for the rest of the family.

The Leal family bartered for food any goods they no longer had use for. Miguel used his skills as a carpenter in exchange for whatever was available in the market of the streets. It was a rough struggle.

David knew his father had worked hard to come up with that sum.

"How are we going to carry the foam slab from here?" Miguel asked the young brown-haired man.

"A man I know is coming with a truck. He's a licensed driver and, though this area is out of his route, no one will question him," Luis answered, jutting his jaw out with confidence.

Miguel shook his head. "I don't like having to tell others about my secret business."

"What else could I do?" asked Luis, throwing his hands up. "I've known the man for some time. Everyone calls him Toro. He's afraid of nothing." He gave a silly nervous laugh.

Toro, the bull. David didn't have a good feeling about a man who had no fears. But, he knew they had little choice. "It would give us away in a minute to be seen carrying this bulky thing through the streets, Papi."

Miguel nodded resignedly.

When they heard the rumble of the truck engine, Luis looked out the dusty window. "It's Toro. Let's load it up and get going."

Father and son picked up the feather light slab and tucked it into the truck. Miguel and Luis piled into the back and held down the block to keep it from bouncing. The men lowered the canvas cover for the back opening and secured it in place.

David volunteered to sit in the cab with the driver. He wanted to keep close tabs on each of the men, who now could hold this incriminating evidence over them.

Toro's wide-set dark eyes didn't ease David's immediate distrust for the man. His thick hair was combed back and flattened by a cap so that the sides bulged out above his ears like horns. David wondered if this was how he got his name. Toro didn't say much. When he did answer David's questions, it was with a disinterested grunt or a simple nod.

They drove down familiar streets and David marveled at how stained and run-down the old buildings looked. It had been years since he had ridden in a motor vehicle and taken the time to look around. He hadn't given it much thought before, but he couldn't remember anyone painting or sprucing up a building in a long time. Electric signs, which had advertised shops and goods in another affluent era, were useless now. No one bothered to make them work again. They had no purpose. Only the murals extolling revolutionary messages were kept in spotless condition.

David cringed at the loud grating of gears in the old Russian truck. He felt very self-conscious and wary knowing he had no legitimate business riding in it. Every face in the street seemed to question his purpose.

When he spotted two uniformed State Security officers standing at the corner of an intersection, David felt hot beads of sweat build up on his forehead. He considered slipping down under the dashboard so he would not be seen, but then realized it would be a stupid thing to do.

"Smile and give them a friendly wave," Toro said through his large teeth.

David noticed that Toro was smiling as if he had no concerns. David did as he was told, though he wondered if his smile looked convincing.

As they approached the armed guards, Toro stopped the truck and let it run on idle. David's heart leaped to his throat. The man was a traitor. He was reporting them after all.

"Keep going! I swear I'll get you if you give us away!" David said through clenched teeth.

Toro didn't answer. He stuck his head out the window and yelled out, "Everything going all right?"

The officers smiled. "I could go for a cup of coffee and a cigar!" said the shorter man. The men laughed hoarsely.

Toro put the engine in first gear and started moving again. He waved and yelled, "You guys have a good night."

As the officers receded in the distance, David turned to Toro. His green eyes blazed with ferocity. "You pull something like that again and I'll make sure you don't walk for a long time!" There was venom in his words.

"You've gotta be cool about these things, *muchacho*," Toro said, glancing at David casually. David didn't like to be referred to as youngster by this man who wasn't that much older than him.

Toro's features were relaxed and unburdened. He winked a dark eye. "You've gotta be friendly with people in the right places." Toro burst out into full-hearted laughter.

Under David's strict and smoldering orders, Toro parked the truck by a concealing tree two blocks from the Leal home. The men covered the foam slab with an old tarp they found in the truck. With David in the lead to scout for signs of danger, Miguel and Luis carried the awkward block to the old garage. David lit the rusty lantern and the men made room for the lightweight yet bulky load.

Taking out his wallet, Miguel counted out two hundred pesos and offered them to Luis.

Luis made no move to take the money. "I want to propose something to you." He shuffled his feet, uncomfortable with his request. "You keep the two hundred pesos. In return, I want a seat on the raft."

David and his father quickly exchanged glances. They felt uneasy about this turn of events.

"I've got to leave here." A vein in Luis' temple filled and pulsed visibly. "I can't go on lying in bed with an empty stomach every night. Who knows where I'll end up, as frustrated as I feel."

"There's not going to be much room. The raft is just for me and my father." David straightened his shoulders and stared unflinchingly at the man's brown eyes.

"Can't you make room for one more? I want to jump off with you," the young man pleaded, using the slang that Cubans had made up to refer to casting off on raft voyages. His eyes darted from father to son. "I'll do my part. I know where I can lay my hands on some canvas, rope and other stuff you'll need."

Miguel gave his son a questioning glance. David shrugged. Supplies were hard to find. Besides, the money Miguel had been able to raise by selling a few things was quickly draining away.

"You've got to pull your load," Miguel admonished. His green eyes were hard. "A lot of lives are at stake here. Not a word about this to anyone!"

"You won't regret it, my friend," Luis said. His lips broke into an open, grateful smile. "You can trust me."

After sealing the pact with handshakes, the joyful man left the old building. He ran down the dark streets to the waiting truck.

"They're building a raft in their garage!" Luis told Toro excitedly. "They said I could jump off with them."

"You got yourself a passport that easily?" the round-eyed man asked, raising a sinister brow.

Luis looked at him puzzled. "I don't have a passport. I didn't think I would need one if I arrived in the United States as a refugee."

Toro laughed. "You've got to keep up with things! A seat on a raft is called a passport these days." He was silent for a moment, then said, "I didn't know you had that kind of money. A passport is expensive."

"Well, I don't have any money." Luis shook his head slowly. "I told them how much I want to get to freedom. And I promised I'd help build the raft." He thought things over for a moment. His brow furrowed and he appeared strangely distressed. "Of course, I'm not supposed to say anything. So pretend I never told you."

Toro's lips curled in a half smile. "Where's my payment?"

Luis' mouth fell open. "I forgot about that. I told them they didn't have to pay me for the foam if they let me go with them." Luis seemed to shrink in the seat. "I don't have a single *peso* to pay you."

Toro started the engine. His face gave no clue to his thoughts. After they drove along for a few minutes, he gave his passenger a side glance. "We'll forget about the money you owe me, Luis. After all, we're friends." He winked a wicked eye in Luis' direction and asked, "Right?"

Luis nodded warily. He couldn't shake the feeling that there was something unsaid behind his words.

Chapter

3

David walked along the jagged limestone shore with assurance. Although he carried fishing line and tackle in a tin bucket and a heavy cast net under his arm, he held his head high and his back straight. He was very aware that Elena followed.

From all appearances, they were off for an evening of fishing. David hoped he would catch a grouper or snook to bring to the family table, but he had come on a more important mission. Lines of concentration marked his brow as he scanned the shimmering water beyond the cove.

Elena stepped gingerly on each rough limestone boulder. Her arms were spread out for balance like an amateur tight-rope artist. A folded towel in her left hand flapped in the salty breeze. From her right hand, a paper bag dangled, storing crackers and a jar of lemonade prepared from fruit growing in her backyard. She had wanted to please him with his favorite food, *picadillo*, the ground beef with tomatoes and raisins that was such a traditional Cuban dish. But the government now replaced their quota of beef with soy bean meal. It looked like ground beef and could be flavored with spices, when any were found, but it always tasted disgusting.

"Keep up!" he yelled back at his pretty companion. "We've got to go to the end, where the water gets deeper." Although he seemed impatient with her, he was glad she had come. The authorities questioned anyone who lingered at a beach. Too many people were taking to the seas, and they had orders to stop them. David thought they would attract less attention as sweethearts on a picnic, and that's what they were now, sweethearts.

She took her eyes off of the rocks for a moment and her lips crinkled into a smile. "I'll catch up."

David selected a flat rock at the mouth of the cove, where he could get a full view of the open water. There were no boats in sight. At his feet, countless minnows darkened the bright green water, dancing in unison as though they were one giant creature.

Setting down his equipment, David filled the pail with salt water. Then, he held the cotton net by its center rope at arm's length. He let the wrinkles hang out of it, pulled down by the lead weights along the net's edge. Satisfied there were no tangles, he brought a section of it to his mouth and bit down firmly. Securing the coil of rope with his foot, he grabbed opposite sections of the round net with each hand so that the heavy woven mesh was extended at three points. With a muscular sideways swing of his body, he tossed it forward, releasing his bite and grip at the same time.

"Great job!" he congratulated himself, inclining his head to ensure that Elena had watched. Her wide open eyes followed the white flying mesh.

Like an enormous spider web, the large net opened into a circle and flew over the waves, landing above the cloud of fish with a bubbly splash. The lead weights sank and came together, enclosing the small minnows in a lacework bag. David pulled the net out of the water, picked out the vaulting silver fish and placed them carefully into the pail.

"Spread the towel on the rock and sit by me," he invited while baiting the hooks with the live prey.

Elena's nose wrinkled with disgust. "How can you do that to those poor creatures?"

Taking the time to cast the lines into the water, he shrugged offhandedly. "You can't be squeamish about these things, Elena. People have to eat." Thoughts of the hunger that often kept him awake at night raced through his mind. He glanced at her from the corner of his eye.

Resting back on her elbows, Elena regretted the paper bag didn't hold a delicacy prepared by her own hands. She understood her mother's pleasure whenever she managed to buy meat or milk on the black market to serve to her family.

Her soft brown hair fluttered in the breeze. David ached to run his fingers through it, but responsibility called. Although his father had a pair of old binoculars, he hadn't risked bringing them. He squinted his eyes and scanned the northern horizon from east to west. A small fishing boat appeared as a dark outline in front of the setting sun. After determining its purpose, he ignored it.

He consulted the watch his father had entrusted to him. It was seven fifty-five. The faint rumble of an engine brought his eyes back up. A well armed gray launch was returning from its rounds on schedule. The Border Guard boat went into port every evening for its crew's leisurely meal. It would be eleven before David would hear the familiar rumble again or see the boat's search lights.

David had been studying the guards' maneuvers and timing their schedule for two weeks now. He had kept the information in his head. It was too risky to write it down. The official vessel kept time like a reliable Swiss watch, making his job easier.

Elena was pensive. She hated to think he would soon be sent to a school in the country. "What is going to happen when you go away? It hurts to think I won't be able to see you whenever I want."

A shocking chill flashed over his neck. How did she know? Heat rose to his temples and his brow furrowed with anger. "Who told you about our raft?"

his voice thundered. "Our trip is none of your business!"

Elena gasped as her mind raced to make sense of his furious words.

"Was it that idiot Luis? It couldn't have been my parents. They never would blab about such a serious thing." David grabbed her arm and pulled her to her feet with a swift jerk. His hot breath scorched her. "Tell me!" he blasted.

On her face was a grimace of alarm. Her stomach clenched like a tight fist. In a small frightened voice, she managed to say, "I didn't know you were planning to go to sea."

"Don't deny it!" he shouted, giving her arm a shake. "You said you feared my going away."

Finding her composure, she wriggled her arm free. "I meant I'd miss you when you went to agrarian service in September."

Now, it was his turn to be stunned. He was rendered speechless. A cold wave washed down his face as the blood drained from his head. He had given away their guarded secret. He alone was to blame. How could he face his father after breaking a sacred pledge?

In the silence broken only by the constant splash of the waves, a growing panic welled in Elena's throat. Hot tears blinded her. "Don't do it, David. Don't jump off. It's too dangerous."

He felt so stupid, like a child one can't trust with a bag of candy. He snapped at her, "Life in Cuba is too dangerous! You have to watch everything you do or say!"

"But a journey on a flimsy raft is like tempting fate!" Her eyes searched his face.

David stared back at her with fire in his green eyes. "My fate here is sealed, Elena. After I get through with Tomás Pico, the man whose cowardice got me in trouble, I'll end up in prison for certain!"

"You haven't done anything yet," she said beseechingly, taking his hands in hers. "There's no need to run. After a while, I'm sure you'll get over your anger."

He shook his hands free, gathering the fingers into angry fists. "Elena, once a finger is pointed at you, State Security keeps an open file. Every move you make is risky!"

She sought his eyes with hers, but he avoided the earnest prayer in them. "The odds on the sea are far greater!"

"If I stay here, I'd have no control over my life. Taking to the sea is a choice I make." Shaking his head with frustration, he yelled, "You're just like my mother. Women can't face the challenges of life."

Tears ran down her pink cheeks. She bit her lip to keep it from quivering. "Is your whole family jumping off?"

"No, Mami won't take the risk. She's staying with Diana." He shook his head. "It's just as well. The trip's too challenging for women."

"What makes you sure it's safe for you?" she asked, her quivering voice full of concern.

"No one's guaranteeing us anything!" he said, annoyed that she wasn't supporting his important plans. "It's a chance a man's got to take for freedom."

"I'm afraid I won't see you again, whether you make it to Florida or not." Her voice trailed off, fearful.

"You really know how to boost my courage." He bit his words, taking out his inadequacy on her. "You are probably right. We might not see each other after this." His words were harsh, but a pang of loss nevertheless tugged at his heart. He spun away from her, facing the endless ocean.

She choked a sob back down to her soul. "Is there anything I can say to change your mind?"

"There's no turning back. The plan is set," he said firmly.

"I've heard of so many people who have died after days at sea." Elena stared through the cloud of moisture in her eyes at the boy to whom she had given her heart. "I don't want you to die."

"We're on the same team then," he said sarcastically, to hide his shame and anger at himself for having blurted out his plans. "You can't change my mind. We're jumping off Tuesday night."

Elena joined him at the edge of the water. She felt his muscles stiffen as she put her arm around him.

"Look, you are not supposed to know about this." His tone was uneasy. He was ashamed to ask for her silence. "Even my little sister has no idea."

She gripped his hand and squeezed it. "David, I would never endanger your life."

<center>~~~~~~</center>

"Look what I found. Miguel, David, come and see!" Luis' shouts made them look up from their work.

Miguel laid down his hammer. David dropped the canvas he was repairing with careful stitches, as Rosa had taught him. They ran outside with nervous curiosity.

With his feet spread apart, Luis held up two red oars. He looked like a scarecrow propped up with stakes. Luis grinned proudly.

"What's the matter with you?" Miguel barked furiously. "Have you lost your wits?"

In three fast strides, father and son were by his side. Grabbing an oar each, they caught Luis by the elbows and dragged him into the garage.

"What are you doing?" Miguel was furious. "Announcing our trip for all the neighbors to hear?"

"But, I didn't say anything about our trip," Luis said, shaking his head innocently.

"You didn't have to," David snapped. "These oars might as well be red banners flashing the news," he said, menacing the thin man with the paddle he still held.

"Your brains must be on vacation." The fire in Miguel's voice was less intimidating. "I can't believe you carried them through the streets in the middle of the day."

"Well, I had to," Luis said with a slight shrug. "They're from the pile of stuff the Border Guard keeps by the boatyard."

"You stole them from the Border Guard?" Miguel and David yelled together.

"Some of the guards went out on patrol. When the guy they left behind went out for coffee, a bunch of us ran to the yard and took some stuff."

"I can't believe you did something so stupid!" Miguel spat between his teeth.

"You said you needed some oars." Luis' eyes opened with wonder.

"I didn't expect you'd steal them from under the nose of the Border Guard!" Miguel shouted.

Luis followed him with his eyes. "Look, stealing from this government is simply getting back what's due us. It's payment for repression," he said sheepishly, trying to convince them.

Miguel threw his hands up in the air. "If anyone followed you here we're dead. They'd have two charges against us: stealing government property and planning to leave the country illegally."

"They'd claim we're enemies of the Revolution, antisocial non-persons. We'd rot in jail!" David's skin crawled, remembering his experience in the hated place.

"Nobody followed me. I'm sure." Luis' eyes pleaded for acceptance. "I kept looking back to check."

"You kept looking suspicious, you mean," David said. "And leading them like a guilty thief right to our home."

"If anyone finds out about the raft, I'll wring your neck!" Miguel promised Luis, encircling an invisible neck with his fingers.

David felt the color of shame creeping to his cheeks. He had let it slip out to Elena.

"No, *mi amigo*," Luis said, waving his hands to dismiss Miguel's concerns. "I wouldn't tell anyone about this," he lied nervously. He hadn't meant to tell Toro. He had simply been too excited to keep the news to himself.

Miguel and David traveled across town, sharing the only bicycle they now had. They took turns lugging each other on a wooden seat Miguel had rigged up behind the regular bicycle seat. It was hard to pedal up and down the low hills, as each man was well built and heavy. By the time they arrived, they were winded and drenched with sweat.

They came to place a long distance call to cousin Gabriel in Miami. To avoid having the call traced to them, they had arranged to use a friend's telephone, far from their neighborhood.

"*Buenas tardes*," said the old woman who opened the door. "I've been expecting you."

"Good afternoon, Isabel," Miguel repeated in turn. "We are grateful for your help."

"Oh, it's nothing." Then, as if suddenly worried about unexpected costs, she raised a questioning eyebrow. "Everything will be charged to Miami. Right?"

"Don't worry about a thing. I'm sure my cousin Gabriel will accept a collect call from me."

With poorly disguised relief on her age-etched face, the old lady motioned them to come into the house. "It's sad to see how many families are split up. So many have gone into exile and left elderly parents and brothers and sisters behind." There was a note of sadness in her words. She clicked her tongue for emphasis, as a rider would do to get his horse going.

David gave his father a cautious look. The conversation was steering too close to their secret plans.

Miguel nodded knowingly. "Yes. Even wives and children are being left behind." Glancing back at David's sweaty face, he reassured his son as well as her. "That doesn't mean they're being abandoned. The husbands send them dollars while they wait for permits for their wives and children to join them."

"¡*Caramba*!" Isabel exclaimed. "I'm forgetting my manners. I'll get each of you a glass of ice water. You look like you swam the Florida Straits! You are drenched and glowing with sunburn."

A wave of apprehension crawled up David's spine. "Does she know about our plans?" he asked when she disappeared into the kitchen.

"I'm sure she doesn't," Miguel said, though he also had found the conversation vaguely disturbing. "This goes to show you how careful we must be in everything we say."

"Get going with the call," David said impatiently. "I want to get out of here."

Placing a call outside the country was not a simple task. Few circuits were available and calls to the United States were routed through a third country, usually Canada. It took hours to get through.

Miguel requested his cousin's number from the operator. The call was finally placed. With the receiver back on the hook, they waited for the operator to call them back once she had a connection. David would have to summon all his patience. This call was their life line.

David let each mouthful of ice water linger in his mouth and savored the refreshing coolness before swallowing. The cold liquid quenched his thirst. He thanked Isabel and sat down by his father. He rehearsed in his head the message they must pass on to Gabriel.

It was not prudent to speak openly over the telephone wire. One was never sure when a line was being monitored. As a necessary precaution, Miguel had devised a code to alert Gabriel of the upcoming plans. He had spelled out the code in a letter and mailed it to his cousin weeks earlier. Although letters leaving the country were at risk of being opened and scrutinized, Miguel had taken the chance.

Their departure was coming up soon. The time had come to let Gabriel know the date.

It had been hours since Isabel had excused herself and gone to bed. She had not offered them dinner, contrary to their generous Cuban custom, because her small rations did not permit her to honor polite traditions. Miguel and David understood and they did their best to ignore the empty feeling in their bellies. David paced the floor of the small living room restlessly. Miguel, dozing on the couch, was startled into a sitting position when the loud ring of the telephone broke the silence.

David rushed to pick up the receiver. "¡*Oigo!*" he called out. "It's the operator, Papi," he said excitedly. "You'd better do the talking."

"This is Miguel. *Sí, sí.*"

David listened anxiously as his father paused.

Moments later, Miguel's face lit up with relief. "Gabriel, my cousin, it's me. Miguel. It's good to hear your voice."

David thought he detected the receiver lightly shaking against his father's cheek.

"Yes. It's one of those things that we all have to go through," Miguel nodded as if his cousin could see him. "Rosa is having her operation on Tuesday, late in the day. She'll have her appendix removed." Rosa wasn't going into the hospital. Miguel was encoding the details of their voyage.

Isabel rushed into the room with the waist cord of her bathrobe trailing behind her on the floor. "Your mother is having an operation?" she asked David in a loud whisper. The hairs on David's neck awakened to attention. The old woman clicked her tongue and shook her head, drawing Miguel's eyes to the darkened corner where she stood.

"Oh, yes," Miguel didn't falter. "But only David and I are allowed to visit her in the hospital. Diana is too young. She couldn't take the experience. She'll look after her mother when she's allowed to go home." Diana and Rosa would be left behind. It was too dangerous for them, he encoded.

"I'll bring over some chicken soup," Isabel said to David in a hushed conspiratorial tone. "She won't be in any condition to be cooking for the family."

David was alarmed, but he managed a weak grateful smile. "I must remember to tell Mami," he said meaningfully.

"I expect she'll be in the hospital three days, maybe four," Miguel continued, giving his cousin an indication of the duration of the journey. Then, a worried look clouded his face. "You've been told it may be a longer stay in the hospital. Six, sometimes seven days?" Miguel had been alerted to new concerns. If the voyage took that long, there could be disastrous results.

"That's what I've heard too. Patients take longer to recuperate. There's so little medicine these days." Isabel's unruly gray hair danced around her head.

"Yes, send us all the medicine you can," Miguel said picking up on Isabel's comment, although their code for medicine referred to help. He hoped Gabriel could notify Brothers to the Rescue, the search and rescue group formed by Cubans in Miami. The group had civilian pilots who regularly searched the Florida Straits in low flying planes for drifting rafts. "We'll be looking out for it."

As David and his father mounted the bicycle for the return trip home, their anxiety exploded in great peals of laughter. They had thanked Isabel for the thoughtful chicken soup they knew they would never taste.

≈≈≈≈≈

The heat in the garage was stifling, even late at night, but the men wouldn't crack the windows open for fear a neighbor would notice the light from the lantern. Only the wide doors were left ajar for ventilation.

David was proud of their work. Though unpainted and obviously assembled from assorted parts, the raft had the looks of a seaworthy craft. The foam block, painted with roofer's tar to keep out the water, had been encased in a protective frame of boards. Miguel had created a point on the frame at one end to serve as a bow and squared it off at the other. They had installed a board as a rowing bench and another at the stern to seat the man at the tiller. They had even managed to find a pole which would serve quite convincingly as a mast. The canvas sail was folded and the mast was lying prone along the length of the raft. It would be secured in place once the raft was underway.

They had stashed securely against the sides of the raft the supplies that would sustain them through the journey. Five plastic jugs, which had been difficult to locate without attracting attention, held about a gallon of water each. A tin was filled with crackers and rock-hard stale bread, which they hoped would keep. A bunch of bananas, though not fully ripened, would not last long in the unprotected conditions of the open sea. They planned to eat those soon. Through a friend who worked in a foreign tourist store, Miguel had gotten a small tin of roasted peanuts and an expensive box of raisins. He feared these would provoke thirst, but they were the only energy inducing food they carried.

Luis had secured his supplies in the raft also. Though he brought water and crackers, Miguel had insisted it was too little and he should plan to bring along more. David and his father anticipated that they would have to share their food with him.

Miguel had put together some fishing line and hooks. He hoped to supplement what little they brought with fish, though he well knew they'd have to eat it raw.

Important papers, addresses, telephone numbers and photographs of Diana and Rosa were carefully protected in multiple layers of plastic. With regret, Miguel glanced at the old compass he had owned since childhood. It was no longer reliable.

Everything was in order. They would jump off the following night. Everyone was prepared. Everyone except Rosa. She had been quiet and morose around them. Yet, she had not raised objections or attempted to persuade them since the night David learned of the trip.

"I brought something for you," Rosa said with little enthusiasm in her voice. She handed them a paper bag.

David took it and looked in it. "There's six little cans of guava juice and two cans of condensed milk," David counted out for the others' benefit.

"These must have cost a fortune!" Miguel exclaimed, thankful that his wife was finally accepting their plan. "Oh, Rosa. The money I left is for you and Diana. Did you use it up for this?"

"No, I didn't." She looked away evasively. "There's something else in the bag."

David reached down into the paper sack and drew out a lightweight object wrapped in tissue. He uncovered it and held up his mother's statue of the Virgin of Charity.

Rosa's eyes looked pained. "She appeared to three shipwrecked sailors in a storm. She guided them to land and became Cuba's patron saint." Rosa encircled David's cupped hands, which held the small statue. Her voice was firm and entreating. "Pray to her. She will take you to safety."

Though David had never made religion a big part of his life, he felt this was a promise he should make.

Miguel's spirits soared. His wife's lack of approval had been all that had held him down. But he worried about her well being until he could send her money from Miami. "Rosa, how did you pay for these things?" he asked softly.

"That's not important. I care only about your journey being safe." As the tears clouded her vision, she turned and walked out.

Miguel's eyes followed her closely. She took each step gingerly to avoid painful stones. She was barefoot. That was it! Rosa had bartered away her treasured leather shoes.

Miguel ran to her side and pulled her close to him. He kissed her softly. "Rosa, I promise, the first thing I'll send you from Miami will be a pair of shoes!"

Chapter
4

David thought dusk would never arrive on this long-awaited Tuesday. Rosa had cooked a heavy meal and the men had devoured it, knowing it would be their last hot food for a while. Three scrambled egg sandwiches were packed for their first morning at sea. They said brief goodbyes. They did not want to be burdened with grief as they set off.

Miguel and David had arranged to meet Luis in the wooded area where they had hidden the heavy raft the previous night. They had moved it using a cart David had made out of the two bicycle wheels. It had been a quiet but difficult procession. The three men pushed and balanced the raft to the hiding place. It had been a wise thing to do. Now, the raft was only half-way to the cove.

They were pleased to see that the raft had not been discovered. There was no sign of Luis. Without pausing, David and his father brushed off the camouflaging branches from the raft. There was little time to spare. They could maneuver the raft to the water only under cover of darkness, so they couldn't have started earlier. Knowing the Border Guard would be on land in only a couple of hours, Miguel wanted to put distance between the raft and the coast before the patrol launch returned for its rounds. Their opportunity to make a clean escape was limited to two or three hours.

As they pushed the heavy load through the woods, they heard the rumble of a motor. The growing noise indicated a vehicle was coming in their direction along the adjacent dirt road.

"Run, Papi! We're doomed!" David yelled, lowering his side of the load to the ground.

"Let's hide, *hijo*! Maybe they're not coming for us."

Perhaps, unknown to them, a land patrol had begun to make nightly rounds. Yet, they both feared the people in the truck had knowledge of their business. After all, few vehicles roamed these parts and their purpose could only be official. In any case, the appearance of a vehicle was a bad omen.

David ran alongside his father to the edge of the woods and they hid behind rocks. His heart pounded in his chest. Having been under investigation by State Security, he knew he wouldn't be given a second chance. His fate would be sealed without question.

They watched as the truck stopped by the place where they had left the raft the night before. David felt his heart jump to his throat. Beads of sweat oozed from his forehead like a soaked sponge that cannot hold any more water.

"I found the raft! Someone moved it!" a voice called out from the darkness.

David looked at his father with apprehension. Though he could hear his short anxious panting, he could not detect Miguel's features in the moonless night.

"I can't find any sign of them. Where are they?" a man asked.

The good meal Rosa had cooked no longer stuck to David's ribs. It was swirling uncomfortably in his stomach.

"David! Miguel!" the man yelled. "Where are you? It's me. Luis!"

"*¡Loco!*" Miguel spat angrily. "The man is crazy! I shouldn't have let him come along!"

"It's just me and Toro. Come on out," Luis yelled in every direction.

Miguel leaped out of his hiding place and lifted Luis by the collar of his shirt. "Do you have an ounce of brains? You are announcing our names out to the world!"

David cut the distance to his father's side in seconds. "We should let you have it!" His fists opened and closed, hungry for vengeance. "How could you bring this man here! This is the most critical part of the plan."

Luis released a choking breath. "It was back-breaking work last night. With Toro here, we can load the raft in his truck and move it to the beach."

Miguel tightened the grip on the man's collar, so that now Luis stood on tiptoes. "¡*Idiota*! Don't you realize how much attention we'll get using a truck? State Security is probably trailing you already!"

"I didn't think of that," Luis said shakily. "I thought it was a good idea, my friend."

Toro, who had relished the uproar while leaning on his truck like an uninvolved spectator, now spoke. "You're wasting good time. You can't undo what's done." He paused to let his words sink in. "Let's get the raft in the truck and get out of here."

Reluctantly, Miguel agreed. He shoved Luis back and released him. "If I take you with us now, it will be as shark bait!"

They made it to the cove in no time at all. Miguel and David split up briefly to look around for signs of danger.

Luis guided Toro as the driver moved the truck into position. They backed the heavy vehicle onto the shore to be able to launch the vessel directly into the water. The wheels gripped the jagged rocky ground, yet, here and there, they traveled over damp sand.

"Back it up. You still have a few yards to the water," Luis directed, fruitlessly twirling his hand in the darkness like a toy windmill.

"There's a rock coming up! Cut to the right!" he called out to the driver.

Toro did as advised, but the left tire mounted the edge of the outcropping and dropped down heavily onto the sand. There was a loud screeching as the rough limestone scraped the underside of the moving truck. "Is that your head I just ran over? It sounded like dense stuff!" Toro shouted and laughed.

"Go forward! No! No! Back up!" Luis hollered, confused. He scratched the top of his head.

The driver couldn't follow the mixed up directions. Toro stuck his head out the window. "You got us stuck on the stupid rock! Jerk!" Toro shook his head, amazed at the witless man.

When he stepped on the gas to get loose of the protruding limestone, the wheels spun. "Now we're buried in the sand up to our arm pits!" Toro rubbed his forehead with his hand. "If this is how you help your friends, I wouldn't want you as an enemy."

Hearing the noise, David and Miguel ran back to the truck.

"What's going on?" David asked. A swift appraising look gave him the answer.

"It's not a big thing," Toro said with a laugh of dismissal. "I got us pretty close to the water."

"The truck is a dead give-away." Miguel shook his head, exasperated. Couldn't they see the significance of their acts? "Once they spot it, they'll be after us."

"If this whole plan gets ruined, I'm holding you responsible." David furrowed his brow angrily and pointed a threatening finger at Luis.

"David! David!" A soft feminine voice fighting the off-shore wind cut short his accusations. "I thought you'd leave before I could get here."

David took a great gulp of air. Elena had come to say her goodbyes. Her presence embarrassed him. Now, his father would know he had been unable to keep a secret. David glanced at Miguel sheepishly.

The girl stopped short of the group. Her slight figure was barely discernible against the dense backdrop of the tree line.

"It's a launching party! Did she bring the champagne?" Toro tilted his head back and let out a satisfying guttural laugh.

"David! You told her!" Miguel exclaimed angrily.

David was glad for the cover of darkness. He was sure the fury in his father's eyes would bore holes into him otherwise. David scaled the jagged limestone in quick strides. Squeezing Elena's elbow in the anger generated by his shame, he dragged her to the woods.

"What are you doing here? This can put us all at risk!" David whispered harshly.

"Oh, David. I just couldn't stay away," her voice was weepy. "I had to see you one last time."

David shifted his weight from foot to foot. Her tears made him feel uncomfortable. He looked down at her haughtily. "Go home, Elena."

Anguished, Elena rested her head on his unyielding chest and covered her face with her hands. Drowned sobs jolted her young body.

David was moved by her sadness. He worried about their safety at sea as much as she did. For days he had held back his feelings to summon courage for the trip. In his fifteen years, Elena was the only girl he had cared about. They would part now, probably forever. David wrapped his arms around her, giving in to his awakened emotions.

"It will just take a few days," he said, reassuring himself as well as her. "I'll write to you when we get there." David felt her head move up and down in agreement.

His hands gently pushed her shoulders away from the warm protection of his chest. He covered her soft mouth with his in a parting kiss. Elena responded hungrily. The touch of her lips was a delicious sensation. Her arms laced around David's neck, lifting her body and holding it tightly to his chest.

"¡*Vamos*, David! Let's go!" Miguel's voice carried over the splashing waves. As if a bolt of lightning had suddenly hit them, the romantic moment ended abruptly.

"I have to run!" David said, planting one last kiss on her smoldering lips. He released her locked arms from his neck and turned to go.

"Wait, David!" she said suddenly, as if startled from a dream. "This is for you."

David took from her hand a small envelope encased in a protective plastic bag. He shoved it into his shirt pocket.

"I'll pray for you!" Elena shouted as he ran back to the others.

"All out of kisses now?" Toro mocked as David rushed past him. "Smack, Smack." Toro teasingly mimicked resounding kisses.

"Cut it out!" David said irritated and then insulted him under his breath, "*¡Estúpido!*"

"Get in the raft before anything else happens!" Miguel commanded.

The homemade vessel had been launched by the three men. With a touch of pride and relief, David noticed that it floated high in the shallow water. Luis and Miguel held the raft upon the waves with one foot in the water and one on board. David climbed in and, taking one of the oars, prepared to push off against the sandy bottom.

In a moment, Toro jumped into the raft and grabbed the other oar. "We're off!" he yelled with gusto, waving the oar above his head.

With the speed of a basketball player jumping for the hoop, Miguel leaped into the raft. Spreading his legs to brace himself on the rocking craft, he came face to face with Toro. "Where are *you* off to?" he asked, bitingly.

Toro was coolly unconcerned. He planted the working end of the oar on the bottom of the raft and held it upright between himself and his angry questioner. "Off to Miami," he said smoothly, savoring each word.

Luis watched bewildered. His one foot in the water scraped the sandy bottom like a living anchor.

David was furious. When he stood up to back up his father, the vessel tilted precariously to one side. He couldn't risk overturning it before they set off. David sat back down.

"You are not invited," Miguel said firmly, balancing himself with ease. Too much rested on this voyage. He didn't want a stranger along.

"I have no choice." Toro pointed his determined chin in the direction of the truck. "I'm in hot water now with a government truck stuck in the sand."

"That's not my problem," Miguel shrugged. "I didn't ask for your help. From the looks of things, I'd say you had planned for this all along."

"Look," Toro said, his voice showing no sign of relenting. "I'm the assigned driver of the truck. I'm accountable for it. What kind of delivery should I say I was making when State Security asks why the truck is stuck in the cove?" In the darkness, David could easily picture the man's protruding eyes squinting with intimidation.

Miguel stood his ground. He wouldn't be bullied into yielding. "Tell them someone stole it from you. You have no idea who did it."

"It seems to me you are a smart man, Miguel."

Miguel cringed imperceptibly when Toro used his name as though they were friends.

"Are you sure you want to leave me behind, disappointed and angry? I'd have to give them something to save my skin." A vindictive threat colored Toro's words.

A current of heat raced through Miguel's veins. He made a move to punch the defiant man. Toro lifted the oar menacingly.

"No, Papi!" David shouted, rising to his feet in the cramped rocking platform. The effort to maintain their balance imposed a momentary truce on the hostile opponents. "Don't let him reduce you to this. He's going to win either way, whether we take him on the raft or not."

Miguel's fist was paralyzed in the ready position. Only the sound of the waves lapping at the sides of the raft could be heard during the silent, anxious wait.

"We have food and water for three. We can't possibly share and survive." Although still incensed, Miguel tried to bring reason back to the fierce argument. "I have to look out for my son and myself. It's a matter of life and death."

"I packed my own supplies." Toro's cold voice chilled David to the soul.

"You shameless scum!" David shouted. "You planned to scrounge a trip to freedom at our expense."

Toro's victorious laughter was a beast's snort, master of his territory.

~~~~~~

Toro and David rowed along side each other. David held in check his scorn and resentment for the man. They had to work together. Rowing required technique and strength. They were the most fit for the job.

Miguel charged himself with maintaining course at the tiller. "We have to get far off the coast in the next few hours," he warned them just loud enough for the men to hear. "If we get past the range of normal patrol for the Border Guard, we have a chance to make it."

Luis, kneeling at the make-shift prow, had the job of look out. Miguel had fastened his old binoculars around the man's neck. Proud to be trusted with the responsibility, Luis took it to heart. He scrutinized the black canopy that engulfed them.

"I don't see a thing!" he exclaimed. "To the south, I see the lights of the city, but that's all."

Toro shook his head without breaking his rowing rhythm. "We've been staring at them since we left! ¡*Estúpido*!"

"¡*Silencio*!" Miguel quieted them with authority. "Sound carries a long distance over water." His tone was harsh but hushed.

"*Sí, Capitán*," Toro ridiculed him.

David took a deep breath to cork his rising annoyance.

"Let's get one thing straight," Miguel whispered calmly. "To make it, one of us has to be in charge. I have the most experience and I've studied every aspect of this venture. I will give the orders." His determination couldn't be mistaken.

"Of course, Miguel," Luis said solicitously. "This is your raft."

"I have no problem with that. Do you David?" Toro's tone bordered on mockery. Toro elbowed his rowing partner. For the sake of peace, David remained quiet and simply rolled his eyes.

"As long as we are within normal patrol distance, I want quiet. The only time we will speak will be to point out any suspicious activity on the water. Understood?" Miguel didn't expect an answer. His question was intended as a threat.

With his arm, Miguel secured the tiller against his side, then wiped his sweaty hand on his pants. Anxiety had brought on the perspiration, not heat or effort. A great weight rested on his shoulders.

"We will all be alert for any sign of the Border Guard. This is hardly a fun afternoon cruise." Although David agreed with his father's proposal, he didn't need a reminder that this was not mindless and fun. His arms ached from supplying the raft's moving power.

Miguel strained to read the luminescent hands of his watch. "At about this time, the launch returns for another shift. We've got to be especially cautious."

"We can't fight them if we see them." Luis' whispered thoughts registered their inability to defend themselves. David wondered if Luis had it in him to do anything about it, in any case.

"We haven't got a chance in the world to fight them." David pursed his lips, annoyed that Luis had to point out something so obvious. "No one's got weapons but the military!"

Miguel continued laying out his orders. "The trick will be to spot the Border Guard, yet make sure they don't see us. Once we know they're out on the water, there will be total silence. Not a word, or a whisper, or even a cough! We will put all efforts into widening the distance between us."

"They have search lights. If they point them at us, even a deaf-mute can't escape," Toro chuckled.

David's skin crawled. Nothing brought fear to the man.

"They'll use them only if something catches their attention," Miguel warned. "I chose tonight because there's no moon to give us away. You can't tell where the ocean ends and the sky begins but for the stars. They won't be able to see our outline."

"We're out past the position of their regular patrol. I'm sure of that," David said knowingly. "This means the shore-bound wind will blow any sound we make in their direction."

"Silence is our only defense, then." Miguel shifted in his seat to look all around. "If they catch wind of us and use search lights, we will sit still as grave stones. Even the rowing will stop."

The men went back to their own troubled thoughts. Invisible waves lapped at the wooden sides of the vessel, occasionally startling the occupants out of any sense of security with cool salty spray. The crew rowed and peered into the darkness. David and Toro huffed with each forward push. It was the only human sound to be heard.

"I see them! Over there!" Luis broke the stillness and pointed frantically to the southeast. "I see their light on the water, where you said they'd come out!"

In a flash, the men's heads spun. Three pairs of fearful eyes strained to focus.

"Be quiet!" David warned with a furious whisper.

"Hand me the binoculars!" Miguel said in a hoarse whisper.

Luis didn't respond. "They're coming for us! I knew this would happen!" His voice rattled with fear.

"Give me the binoculars!" Miguel ordered.

"They're setting a fire! What kind of weapon is that?" Panic gripped Luis' voice. He made no attempt to release the glasses.

"David! Grab the binoculars from this *loco*!" There was no mistaking the ire in Miguel's tone.

"They're finished! They're going up in flames!" Luis stood up and cheered foolishly. The raft rocked and he stumbled, falling hard onto the rowing bench.

David clenched his teeth and threatened, "If you don't shut up, I'll hold your loud mouth under water and let you tell it to the barracudas!" Securing his oar with his knee, David grasped the man's hair. He pulled Luis' head back, grabbed the binoculars and yanked the cord over his head. He released Luis and handed the binoculars to his father.

Focusing, Miguel studied the bright glow. "It's a poor old shrimper. Just a one man skiff with a platform for the fire." Miguel closed his eyes and took a slow, patient breath.

"That's how they attract the shrimp to the boat to net them," David said, disgusted with his fellow rafter. "Don't you know anything?"

"Keep rowing," Miguel directed. "We have no time to waste."

"Maybe the shrimper heard your cries for help and he'll take you away to the safety of our country," Toro teased Luis with his cruel humor.

David hoped that Toro was mistaken, that the fisherman had not heard the commotion. Fishermen could barely scrape together a living. The man could well be inclined to turn them in to the patrolling Guard for a reward.

"There they are," Miguel whispered ominously. "Finally back to their cursed rounds."

The awaited menace had finally appeared. In the distance, a light traveled on the water east of the shrimp boat. The men's eyes followed the course of the bright floating dot. The light moved toward the west, parallel with the coast.

Had it not been the symbol of a dreaded sinister enemy, David would have admitted there was beauty to the streaking spark. Fine luminous fingers radiated from an intense central glow. The brightest stars in the sky did not match its radiance.

The Border Guard launch kept a steady, fast pace as it approached the orange glow of the shrimp boat. Then, as the two lighted objects met, their radiance seemed to merge, the brighter intense beam of the launch taking on a warmer hue.

"What do you make of that, Papi?" David asked, worried.

"They must be checking out the fisherman," Miguel replied, his eyes glued to the enhanced view he had through the binoculars. "Keep a steady pace," he reminded the oarsmen. "Don't let up on the rowing."

"Maybe that's no fisherman," Toro sneered with a note of amusement. "Maybe they're using him as a look out or a spy, searching for unsuspecting rafters."

David wondered if Toro was attempting to drive Luis into the depths of panic, or if he sought to plant fear in all of them. Didn't Toro have respect for brutal authority, even when the reality of it stared him in the face?

"That big bonfire blinds the shrimper to everything beyond its illuminating range," Miguel pointed out, dampening Toro's fun. "He'd make a very inept spy. Keep in mind our voices can carry a long ways. Let's keep it down."

As the rafters watched, enraptured with apprehension, the light sources cleaved once more, taking on their separate identifying glows. The orange light remained in its steady position. The radiant clear beam continued its journey west. As the light diminished and ultimately disappeared, the sweat-drenched men drew a sigh of relief together.

"We'll take a turn at the oars now," Miguel suggested. "I want you to take the tiller, David. Toro, change places with Luis and keep a keen eye all around."

"*Sí, Capitán.*" There was an edge of malice in Toro's tone.

Miguel adjusted his rowing power to the weaker pace of his partner. If he didn't keep the rowing in balance, they would go in circles all night.

Toro glanced around. Seeing no changes in the infinite darkness, he shrugged and stretched his sore arms. He had managed to get away! The way his girl had scorned him, he had feared the police would learn his identity at any moment. He winced with hurt when he thought of Mirta. If they had caught him, he would have spent the rest of his youth in prison, along with Pepe Alonso.

Toro wondered if Miguel and David would have pushed him off the raft if they knew who he was. He knew he would have to take great care not to slip up.

Toro saw no need to keep a lookout when the Border Guard was searching the waters miles away from their position. Miguel was being overly cautious. Even if they spotted the bright light again, there was little to be done. The others could do his job just as well. Toro rested his head on the side of the craft. He closed his eyes and within minutes was sound asleep.

"Aim for the North Star, *hijo,*" Miguel reminded David softly.

Chapter

5

As the light of a new day evolved from dimmest gray to glorious brightness, David took in the vast expanse of ocean that surrounded them. All around, the water heaved and swelled without breaking its glassy surface. The color of the ocean had changed to a deep dark blue, very different from the shades of blue-green of his land-bound experiences with coastal waters. He imagined the intense color was an indicator of great depth, and he stared into the crystalline void, fascinated. The water rose in an undulating movement, and David was amazed at the gelatinous quality of the water's dance. It was then he became aware of the first signals of discomfort. His head buzzed. His stomach seemed to swim. The unceasing movement was playing dirty tricks with his balance.

David looked up from the unsettling movement of the water. He would have to concentrate his mind on something else. He was satisfied to see the intensely orange rays of the sun reaching up from the eastern horizon. With the rising sun on starboard, the bow was indeed facing north, the proper direction for the start of their venture.

Glancing around at his companions, he nodded a quiet "good morning" to his father. Miguel leaned his head over the side of the raft and inspected its condition. Looking back at his son as they traded places to check the port side, Miguel raised his brows in approval.

"It's holding up," he whispered, smiling broadly. "I'm very surprised."

"I'd be surprised if it came apart," David said seriously. Currents of dread raced from his chest. "Coating the foam with roofing tar was genius at work, Papi. You should be proud to have come up with a way to keep it from soaking up water."

Miguel shrugged modestly. His calm looks masked the uncertainty he felt about the reliability of his design.

Luis slept, his legs bent together close to his abdomen. Though he looked peaceful, David knew the man had not rested well. Sleep was difficult in the tossing raft. The space was cramped and wet. David himself had managed only a few minutes of uneasy slumber when he was released from his turn at the oars. Even so, he didn't begrudge the thin man his needed rest.

David's eyes traveled to Toro, who sat across the raft from him. The man's thick hair stood out above his ears, dry and stiffened by the salt spray that had drenched it the night before. Now that David saw him in the light of day, he noticed that his eyes were large and round, rimmed with long black lashes. His gleaming gaze seemed to hold back anger on the verge of explosion. His nose was straight and wide and his jaw square and strong. David could see the resemblance to a furious penned bull and wondered if Toro got pleasure from being known by his nickname.

Toro's menacing eyes were fixed on David. A shiver of hate ran down David's spine, yet he controlled his muscles to show no emotion. Toro seemed to thrive on making people uncomfortable in his presence. David wouldn't feed the man's need.

Miguel reached for the plastic bag that protected their morning meal from the salt spray. He untied the string that had secured it to a wooden beam throughout the night.

In his relaxed sleep, Luis took in a whistling breath and released it with a sonorous repetitive flapping, the drumming of exhaled air on the loose tissue of his throat. All eyes went to the sleeping form. Miguel chuckled and glanced at his son, sharing his amusement.

Toro's brows came together, giving his wide eyes a look of great annoyance. He sat up straight. Swiftly, his leg contracted and shot out. Luis was jerked awake as Toro's foot landed on the prone man's rump. Luis blinked his eyes. He attempted to get his bearings after the sudden disruption of his slumber. Toro laughed heartily.

"Why did you do that?" David yelled angrily. "The man was sound asleep!"

"It's daylight," Toro said, shrugging. "Is he going to sleep all day?"

"We need all the rest we can get," Miguel said. "It doesn't matter how or when we get it." His voice was appeasing. Though he was still angry at Toro for forcing his way into the raft, he knew their quarters were too confined to fight.

"He's just being lazy." Toro smiled at Luis, who now stretched and yawned.

"What do you expect him to do instead?" David asked with acid in his words.

"For one thing, he can row." Toro's brows went up in challenge. "We've got to keep moving."

"We *are* moving," Miguel said emphatically. He dug inside the breakfast bag, unraveling layer after layer of plastic which Rosa had insisted on to keep the water out.

"We are swaying up and down." Luis looked at Toro as if puzzled that the man had not noticed.

David shook his head. Luis had missed the point. "We are being carried toward the Gulf Stream. We are drifting slowly, whether we try or not."

"That's right, very slowly," said Miguel, still busy with the breakfast bag.

"You mean, the current is going to take us to Florida?" Luis asked incredulously.

"If we're lucky. The Gulf Stream is like a wide flowing river." Miguel glanced at Luis, whose eager eyes masked his lack of sleep. "Could be that it takes us to Cay Sal or some other little island in that bank."

"We'd reach land. That's great!" Luis said hopefully.

Miguel shook his head. "We couldn't stay there. We would only rest for a while then set off again."

"Those islands are deserted. There's not even fresh water," David explained.

"I've heard the Border Guard makes secret raids on the islands," Toro added, not willing to take the chance. "They take back any Cuban they find."

"But those islands belong to the Bahamas! They're not only outside Cuban waters, they're invading another country!" David glanced at his father, expecting he'd dismiss such an outrageous story. Miguel looked down, unable to meet his son's eyes.

Toro shrugged. "They don't care about that, as long as no one else catches them doing it."

Miguel handed his son an egg sandwich. This kind of talk could dampen everyone's spirit. He wanted to give them something positive to hang on to. "We're going to work with Nature. That's why I rigged up a mast and sail. We are not going to rely on ocean currents only."

"Yeah! We don't want to drift for days before we reach land," Toro added. "I've heard of rafts washing up on shore with people baked by the sun like crisp pork rind. They'd had no water to drink for days."

David stared at Toro through lids that were tight slits. The man was smiling wickedly at Luis. David was appalled. How could Toro nurture fears in the weaker man? They were barely starting the journey and there was no turning back.

Toro had earned his name with his ornery nature, David was now sure. The physical resemblance to the beast was only incidental.

Alarmed at Toro's mean streak, Miguel made a big fuss about eating their breakfast. He placed a sandwich on his lap and handed the last one to Luis. "I don't have any breakfast for you," he said to Toro, with little sympathy. "I hope you came well prepared."

Taking the offered food in his hands, Luis looked around at his companions. In the tense moments that followed, Miguel and David kept their heads down, intent on unwrapping their meals. Toro leaned back. He dug into a sack and brought out a large round cracker.

Luis watched as the man studied his dry wafer and wiped the blackened crumbs that clung to the underside. Wracked with guilt, Luis called out to him, "Save it for later. You can have half of my sandwich."

David and Miguel looked up surprised. Luis gently tore the bread, soft and somewhat soggy from the moisture of the eggs. Toro took the food without a moment's hesitation. If he was grateful, it was evident only by the ravenous bite he immediately took.

Luis earned a notch of esteem from David. Despite his slow wit and the abuse he got for it, Luis had a generous heart.

David rearranged the scrambled eggs, which squirted out of the soggy bread as he squeezed it. The food didn't appeal to him as he had hoped it would when his mother had prepared it. As he brought the sandwich up to his mouth, the smell of the cooked eggs reached his nose. His stomach squirmed and knotted. He lowered the food back onto his lap.

David took a deep breath and tried to distract his mind from the unpleasantness building up in his stomach. He stared at the sky. He was surprised there wasn't a cloud in sight. The dome above them was a pure and crisp light blue. The sun was now a round globe of blinding light hovering just above the line of the horizon.

"You should make an effort to eat, *hijo*," Miguel broke into David's thoughts with bull's eye intuition.

"Even the smell of it turns my stomach," David said, and looked across the cramped space in time to see Toro's lips curve into a smirk.

"We've got to keep up our strength," Miguel insisted.

Luis chewed slowly. Discomfort marked his bony face. His brow was pale and damp.

"I'm afraid if I force myself to eat, I might not be able to keep it down," David said, unhappy with himself.

"If it's going to go to waste, I'll eat it!" Toro was ready to benefit from the opportunity.

Miguel raised an eyebrow in warning. "Keep your dirty hands off his food!" Then, taking another bite of his own sandwich, he turned to his son. "Why don't you try to eat half? Put the other half in the bag for later."

"I'll try," David answered, unconvinced.

He chewed the first few morsels and they were quickly drenched in a puddle of spit. His jaw felt heavy and he had great difficulty swallowing. His head seemed to wobble without control, in time to the dance of the heaving sea. He felt great drops of sweat build up on his upper lip. In spite of the tightness in his abdomen, he followed his father's advice. He knew weakness and dehydration were two of their principal enemies.

He finished the first half of the meal, as he had committed to do. He rewarded himself with a sip of water to wash it down and remove the offensive taste from his mouth. Now, the battle began to keep his stomach from returning the meal. David took in deep breaths. The air was warm and salty.

Noticing his distress, Miguel put his son to work. He had to find a way to distract him. In fact, he was also feeling the initial dizziness and uneasy stomach that signaled a bout of sea sickness.

"Give me a hand with the sail," he said to David firmly. "There's a slight breeze and we're going to capture it."

David leaned forward, glad to be useful, yet suffering with every movement of his body.

"Pull on the line while I straighten the sail." Miguel kneeled on the seat and, holding on to the welded steel mast, attempted to stand. The vessel leaned to the side.

"¡*Aayyy*! My belly's jumping around!" Luis yelled. His arms wrapped around his middle.

"Take it easy, Luis," Miguel said. "I'll just be a moment."

While David pulled up the sail, Miguel guided it up the mast. As the heavy canvas triangle filled with air, the unattended boom swung dangerously close to Luis' head.

"Duck your head!" David warned. Quickly, he reached for the rope trailing from the boom.

When Luis suddenly doubled up to avert the swinging boom, he went into spasms of nausea. "I'm going to puke! I can't stand it anymore!"

"Quit announcing your illness. Nobody wants to hear about it," Toro hollered, holding the tiller.

Miguel, knowing first hand the welling discomfort the poor man was experiencing, was gentle with him. "Take a few deep breaths and try to think of something else."

"I can't think of anything else but my heaving stomach," Luis moaned.

"You've got to keep it to yourself. We feel just as sick," David assured him.

"Not me," Toro advertised grandly. "I'm just as fresh as a bowl of lettuce."

The mention of food drew another anguished moan from Luis, but he didn't voice his distress this time.

David's irritation with Toro simmered. He tied the rope and watched the sail tighten and hold. His father gingerly returned to his seat and took the tiller from Toro. Miguel's look of satisfaction at the performance of his homemade rig was marred by a green specter on his face. David recognized it as the color of sickness. His father suffered, too.

David examined Toro with scorn. It seemed ironic that those who had labored and risked so much for this trip were brought to their knees with nausea. The freeloader looked as happy as if he were sailing for fun with his girl.

David was proud of his father. Miguel had the ability to construct a craft worthy of the sea. Granted that it wasn't much to look at, but it was sturdy. Miguel had learned his trade from his father, a carpenter. He had also made use of his knowledge of plumbing and welding in rigging it securely. What amazed David most was how easily his father took to the sea. He navigated with ease and, though he didn't have his sea-legs yet, he led the crew with authority.

To fight off his swirling stomach, David stared at the sky and concentrated on thoughts that would set aside his discomfort. He tried to recall pleasant memories other than food. He drifted away with thoughts of Elena. Just as he had during the uncertain and fearful nights he spent in jail, he formed a picture of her face in his mind. Her dark eyes rimmed with long black lashes beckoned him. He yearned to touch her soft brown hair. He could still feel the warmth of her lips in their parting kiss. Hers had been the last touch, the last secure memory of firm ground.

Her voice called out to him. Yes, he remembered. She had called him back. She had handed him a small, stiff envelope which he had, without thought, placed in his pocket. Now, he retrieved it and hurried to open it.

As a parting gift, she had given him a black and white portrait of herself. Her smile was soothing and, though there were no tears in her eyes, he imagined this was the way she looked this very moment.

~~~~~~

At the cove, Elena searched the beach from the cover of the tree line. There was no one in sight this clear sunny morning. The tide had come in and the waves broke against the open back of the stranded truck.

She ran down over the rocks to the edge of the water and peered into the cab. Elena was dismayed that it was empty. She asked herself, what did she expect to find? Did she think David had changed his mind and turned back?

She scanned the waters as far as her vision allowed. The raft was gone. Elena didn't know if this was a sign of success or of tragic failure. She pictured David drifting on a flimsy floating tomb. The moisture rimming her eyes seemed to merge with her vision of the ocean, so that she felt her hopes were also adrift on the endless expanse of water. She stared out to sea, quietly giving in to her sorrow.

The rumbling of a motor suddenly alerted her. A vehicle in these parts could only be State Security. Elena didn't want to answer questions that would endanger David. She ran back to the dense cover of the woods. Her heart racing, she peeked from behind the shrubs.

"There it is!"

"I told you the report was true! Someone abandoned a truck in the cove."

Five uniformed men swarmed around the abandoned vehicle. Elena shrank back behind the green covering. Her knees felt like cooked macaroni; they wouldn't hold her up. Her heart thundered in her chest so loud she thought she could hear it. She hoped David and his father were far enough away.

"They've taken off in a raft!"

"Alert the Border Guard! Tell them what we found!"

~~~~~~

David turned over Elena's photograph and found a short dedication in her unmistakable feminine script. *"To David, the bravest man I know. I will always love you. Elena."* As an afterthought, yet meant as a desperate demand, she had added, *"Write to me!!!"*

As he basked in the warmth of her loving words, the grating of Toro's nasty laughter brought him back.

"So that's the little lady that came to see you off. She's quite a pretty morsel." Toro licked his lips in exaggerated provocation. "If we hadn't left, I'd be knocking on her door this very evening."

David flipped the photo back to face him, annoyed that he had unwittingly showed Elena's portrait to the man. "Don't you get me riled up!"

"Jealous?" Toro taunted, drawing his lips into a deriding gesture. "Green as you are in the face, you threaten to mess with me?"

"You're the one who's jealous! With your wild hair and nasty ways, no woman would ever give you a second look."

"I have my ways with women." Though Toro's self assured smile lingered, it looked as though it was pasted on. David felt there was something on the subject Toro was leaving unsaid.

"Sure! I bet they were all lined up to say their farewells. And now they're throwing a good riddance party in your honor." David attempted a weak smile in spite of the terrible dizziness that enveloped him.

"Get off my back!" Toro yelled. It hurt to think how Mirta had turned on him. It seemed you couldn't trust people in Cuba anymore.

David swelled with satisfaction, knowing he had somehow hit a sensitive nerve in Toro.

"What *are* you doing?" Toro yelled, taking his anger out on Luis.

Luis leaned over the side of the raft, holding on to a string.

"You don't think you're going to catch any fish with that, do you?" Toro asked him nastily. "Did you bring along some bait?"

Luis was evasive. "No, I didn't bring any bait."

"You're not wasting good food to feed the fish, are you?" Suddenly protective of his provision sack, Toro accused him, "Did you get something out of my bag?"

"I didn't touch your bag. I promise." Luis' brows angled in a mixture of apprehension and nausea. Crawling over the feet of the others, he tied the string to a beam on the stern.

"Then, what are you trolling with?"

"I'm not fishing." Luis avoided his questioner's eyes and went back to his position on the bow.

"What in the world are you doing?" Toro reached over forcefully and pulled on the string, hand-over-hand.

"No! Leave it alone!" Luis lunged and landed on his tormentor. The raft rocked.

"Let him be!" David yelled at Toro.

"Stop it! You're going to make us capsize!" Miguel hollered with great concern.

Toro wasn't dissuaded. He yanked on the string faster.

Luis grabbed the man's arms in a feeble attempt to stop him. "Let go of it! Don't pull it in!" Luis screamed.

The end of the string was now visible as a red and white form bouncing in and out of the water as it approached the raft.

"Well! Look what I caught!" Toro said holding the small plastic figure out of Luis' reach. Luis clung to the man's arm trying to pull it down. "It's a statue of St. Anthony tied around the feet."

"Give it to me! It's got to be in the water. It can't be taken out until we reach land."

Toro laughed, clearly amused. "You've got your superstitions confused. St. Anthony doesn't save castaways. You put his statue upside down until he finds you a sweetheart."

"Maybe if you had practiced that old superstition, you'd have a sweetie to worry for you," David said, rubbing salt on Toro's touchy wound.

"Hand it back!" Luis moaned.

"Would you let him do what he wants?" Miguel yelled roughly.

Toro seemed to lose interest. He lowered his arm and Luis snatched the statue from his hand.

The statue bounced around in Luis' nervous hands. He leaned over the side and released it, to trail once again behind the raft. But the struggle had caused too much excitement to his system. As he brought his head back up, the contents of his stomach surged up. The soggy chewed food and digestive juices jetted out of his mouth and onto his lap, spraying Toro with the rancid mess.

"You disgusting toad!" Toro exclaimed, revolted. He wiped his pant legs, but raising his hands to deposit the smelly stuff over the side, it seeped through his fingers, further covering his clothes.

Luis' mouth was shaped into a silent scream. He coughed and gagged, bringing up the dregs at the bottom of his belly. His skinny frame shuddered and convulsed.

"I ought to throw you over the side," Toro threatened, reaching for salt water to cleanse the repulsive mess which covered him.

To his dismay, David caught a view of the dense yellow and white glutinous matter shimmering in Luis' lap. He swore to never eat rice pudding again, as it reminded him of the dessert. But, it was the clear secretion which dribbled from Luis' chin, stretching its viscous droplet and springing back, that did David in.

His jaw ached and saliva gushed into his mouth. His stomach churned in revolt. The uncontrollable tide of vomit rose up in his throat. In a swift motion, he spun and spewed his regurgitation into the sea.

Miguel was not spared his turn. He leaned over the side and threw up. When his stomach ceased its spasmodic surges, Miguel reached into the dark water and refreshed his sweaty face. He scooped salty water into his mouth to replace the bitter taste and spit it out.

"Wipe yourself with this," he said, handing an old rag to Luis, who lay spent and shivering.

Exhausted, David avoided the sight of Luis scrubbing himself off. He leaned back, his head spinning.

"Drink some water, *hijo*. You've got to replace what you lost." Miguel measured a small amount into a tin cup and brought it to his son's lips. "Do the same, Luis. You can't afford to be dehydrated this early on the trip." Contrary to the advice he gave the others, Miguel avoided taking a drink. He was angry at himself for wasting the moisture his system needed in one uncontrollable ejection. He feared using up their water too soon and felt a great responsibility toward his son.

Toro removed his shirt and pants and rinsed them over the side. Wringing them, he stretched the wet clothes over the rowing bench to dry. Then, taking a sip of his own water bottle, he sprawled out and let the sun's rays bathe his tanned body. He closed his eyes to avoid seeing Luis, who still worked to wipe off the stinking remains and occasionally moaned in discomfort.

After putting away the cup, Miguel made his way back to man the tiller. His head bobbed and he felt weak. But he was still in charge.

They would make it. He had to believe they would. He was disappointed that he felt so weak so early on. The ocean was calm, Miguel reminded himself. Yet, he hadn't counted on the surging swells of the open water and the havoc the rising and falling can wreak on one's sense of balance. What would become of them if a squall raised the seas into angry peaks? His knowledge of boating was minimal. He had taken a few boat rides during his youth. Although he had not let on to David, Miguel had never left sight of land before.

Afraid to offend a higher power, Miguel dug out the statue of the Virgin of Charity from a plastic sack. Rosa had entrusted their lives to her. Who was he to scoff at her protection? In the vastness of the open seas, Miguel was willing to summon any help he could get. Perhaps the Virgin would team up with Luis' St. Anthony and see them through. Miguel chuckled and glanced over his shoulder at the trailing line. What he saw, raised the hairs on his neck to alert formation. His eyes opened wide.

"We're being followed," he whispered.

David knew they were still close enough to the range of the Border Guard. There was nothing to do. Besides, he was too weak. Sick as he felt, he would almost welcome the arrest. At least he'd get back to dry land.

Toro lifted a lazy eyebrow. He followed Miguel's steady stare. Breaking the surface like a sharp cleaver, a menacing fin followed their course. Toro bolted upright.

"Look who you invited by tossing your chum into the water!" Drawing the attention of the sick men, Toro laughed.

David watched with misgiving. The sides of the raft were low in the water. A careless move could send them in to tangle with the dangerous predator.

"¡*Tiburón*!" Luis yelled loudly, as though his companions hadn't noticed the presence of the beast. He shook, and David wasn't sure if it was from weakness or fear. "He's moving fast! He's coming closer to the raft!"

"Don't worry, Luis," Toro mocked. "You don't have enough meat on your bones for him. He's after St. Anthony!"

"He can't eat the saint!" Luis screamed frantically. The whites of his eyes stood out against the darkly rimmed lids. "St. Anthony will deliver us to safety! If the shark takes him we're doomed!"

Chapter

6

David could not recall a darker, more dreary night than the one they had just been through. There had been no moon. The glorious display of the Milky Way and the constellations his father had pointed out did not replace the complete isolation they felt in the silent darkness. If anything, the celestial dome increased their feeling of insignificance in the vast deserted expanse.

At times he could hear the others' noisy breathing as they yielded for a few moments to the solace of sleep. Mostly, anxiety and fear kept them awake.

The persistent shark had followed the flimsy craft throughout the day. Though Miguel and David did their best to reassure the greatly frightened Luis, David could not deny that the animal's presence caused him much alarm. Since the beast had kept pace with them in the sunlight, David was sure it was still keeping them company in the night. He had read that sharks were attracted by smell and vibrations and not by sight. If this was true, then the absence of light would not deter it from following its prey.

Even so, when the sun illuminated the eastern sky with radiant orange light, David felt a measure of comfort. At least he could see what he was up against. But his reprieve was only in the heart, as his body suffered constant abuse. Within minutes, the sun's powerful warmth set a new fire to his sunburned skin.

"He's still after us! He won't tire out!" Luis yelled anxiously when he spotted the tapered form in the smooth wake that marked the movement of the raft. His screams brought Toro back from a brief rest.

"I bet he's been following us all night," David said, confirming his suspicions.

"He won't give up until we throw you overboard! You wake me up like that again and I'll do it!" Toro threatened Luis.

"Just try it. You'll have to deal with me!" David's teeth clenched tightly.

"Oh, really?" Toro challenged with an indolent smile. "What are you going to do about it?"

"I'll shove you into the sea! If anyone deserves that fate, it's you!"

A wave of fear flooded through Toro. "You don't scare me!" he shouted, but he wondered if David would carry out his threat if he knew Toro's secret.

"No one's going to force anyone off! We've got to stick together." Miguel's words carried power, but his voice lacked its earlier strength.

Beads of sweat had gathered on Luis' sun-burned forehead. He kept anxious watch on the end of the trailing string, which broke the surface like a flirting fishing lure. David wondered if his overheated head looked as inflamed as Luis'. The merciless sun had baked every inch of exposed skin on the floating crew. David's face and neck were painful and hot. The hairs on his forearms were bleached like miniature golden palm trees on a crimson beach. The skin on the back of his hands was red and tight from swelling. The sea spray had evaporated, leaving a dusting of salt on his skin, which sparkled in the brightness.

David had worked and played in the tropical sun all his life. He had never given much thought to its effects. He tanned easily and was proud of the healthy glow he usually displayed. But the relentless burning they suffered was different.

As the day wore on, there was no relief, no place to escape it even for a minute. The sun's midday brilliance had always seemed glorious. Today, it was simply cruel. Even the dancing shadow of the flapping canvas sail, which for a while sheltered his legs, was now a useless sliver.

Ensuring the predator was at a safe distance, David dipped a cup in the ocean and, leaning back, dribbled the cooling liquid on his scalp.

"David, take my cap," his father insisted as he had earlier in the day. They had planned to bring hats, but somehow David's had been left behind.

"I can't take it from you, Papi." He filled the cup again and poured the water over his neck. The coolness was soothing but the relief was fleeting.

Summoning strength, Miguel leaned forward and, adjusting his cap to fit David, placed it on his son's head. David pushed his arm away, resisting weakly.

"We'll take turns wearing it," Miguel said. "I've had it on all day."

Accepting it with a touch of guilt, David smiled. "You don't have as much covering up there as I do. Pretty soon you'll have to wear a cap all the time just to hide your bald head."

"It runs in the family, son. Don't start feeling too smug. Your hair will thin out when you get to be my age." Miguel's chuckle was a rasping sound.

David tilted the brim of the cap so that it covered his eyes. The resulting shade was a sweet gift, although it was a few moments before his vision adjusted to the change.

It was evident that Toro had planned to join the escaping rafters all along. He had given thought to items that would be of use during the ordeal. From his canvas bag, he took out a wide-brimmed hat made from dried palm fronds, typical of the kind that Cuban peasants wore. It protected the man's entire head and covered parts of his shoulders. Miguel's sport cap shielded only the scalp and the eyes. They would have fared better with peasant *sombreros*, David thought with regret.

David was surprised at the weakening effects the environment had on the men in such a short time. Though he was thankful for the calm seas, his head seemed to bob up and down with each movement of the raft, bringing on a dizzy discomfort. He had no appetite. He knew they must keep up their strength, as weakness had already worn them down.

Not Toro, though. He did not seem affected by the sea sickness which had gripped the other three. He had kept quiet most of the morning. He sat sprawled against the side of the vessel with his head held up. Every few minutes, Toro scanned the horizon. He seemed to do this out of a sense of boredom, rather than from anticipation of spotting anything of interest.

David thought fate could not have thrown them a less desirable companion for the trip. Toro had not contributed to the secret, carefully designed plans. He had forcefully demanded a seat without deserving it. David resented this. He was angry that they had been trapped into accepting the rapacious man's demands.

Toro's hostile eyes met David's, jolting his pulse. David held the belligerent gaze, clenching his teeth to suppress his resentment. Toro had less right to the craft than any of the others, yet he didn't seem to suffer.

Toro's lips curled up in a confident grin. A gap marred a straight line of yellowed teeth. The absent tooth was one of his upper canines. Its pointed mate, hanging slightly lower than the others, carried a double job of intimidation.

"He's gone under!" Luis' scream broke the eye challenge. "I can't see him anymore!"

The gray fin had disappeared. The base of the statue of St. Anthony raised a translucent feather of water as it was tugged along by the string.

"He's coming for us!" Luis' voice quavered with fright. "He's gone deep down and he's going to jump up to reach us!"

David pictured the creature jumping out of the water like the trained dolphins he had seen on television. He pulled down the brim of the cap to conceal the amusement that washed over his face. He didn't want to humiliate Luis.

"He's not going to do that." Miguel spoke as if to a child, softly and patiently.

"No," Toro said dragging out his words slowly. His hands imitated the graceful curving of the shark in motion. "He's hiding under the raft waiting to take a bite out of your behind!" With hands forming a large fish's jaw, the fingers snapped together once, rapidly. Toro's eyes squinted wickedly behind the snapping hands.

Luis' wild eyes darted from the man to the water lapping against the sides.

"He can't break through. You know how strong we built the bottom," Miguel reassured him from his prone position.

"But there's holes in the bottom!"

"That's to drain the water, so we don't fill up and sink." Miguel's eyes closed tiredly.

"Besides, it's not likely a shark would do that. They don't behave that way." Glancing at the laughing Toro, David lowered a brow in warning. "Cut it out!"

Toro took pleasure in nagging and irritating Luis, who was too candid and gullible to fight him off. Perhaps that was Luis' salvation. In such confined quarters, Luis' innocent nature might be the shield needed against the testy harassment.

Luis slipped an oar from the rope ring, which, hooked on a wooden stake, served as an oarlock. He held it out over the water as a weapon from the unseen enemy. "I'll crush his head and get rid of him!"

"Put it down, Luis" Miguel said. "You won't even crease his hide with that."

"We've got to do something! He's going to come back!"

"He's not going to get us unless you capsize the raft with all your jumping around." David reached across, attempting to take the oar from the frightened man.

Toro's laughter grated on David's ear. How could the man be amused when Luis' action was endangering them? "See if you find it as funny when the oar falls into the water. I'll volunteer you to swim out to get it," David threatened.

A beam of light glinted from Toro's knife, sending a shaft of dread down David's spine.

Deliberately, Toro sliced a smooth skinned green lime and brought it to his lips on the tip of the blade. There, he squeezed the clear tart juice onto his tongue. David didn't know how to take things in stride. To survive this journey, one had to ease up. Toro's lids lowered and came up slowly, the dark eyes setting on David. "You take things too seriously. A little fun helps pass the time."

"I take *life* seriously." David's burning skin ached as his brows drew close together.

Toro shrugged. "Then let Luis protect us." He threw his head back giving full vent to his laughter.

"He's putting us in danger. I can't find anything funny about that." David's voice resounded with frustration. The man would not participate in responsibility.

Heading off the argument, Miguel suggested David eat something.

"I can't even look at food."

"Me neither," Luis commiserated, lowering the oar while warily keeping an eye on the water. "I feel like a pregnant woman, queasy and tired."

"How would you know how a woman feels?" A puff of air blew out of Toro's flaring nostrils.

"This is what it's like, I'm sure. Without the big round belly, of course." Luis patted his flat middle. "I've heard about their complaints."

Miguel brought his weary body up. "Let's start eating the bananas. The heat is turning them dark." With little effort, he removed one for Luis and as an appeasing gesture he handed one to Toro. Seeing the condition of the fruit, Miguel knew they would not keep much longer.

David hid the disgust that his father's generous action brought on. He twisted a mottled banana from the bunch and peeled it with little enthusiasm. The aroma of the fruit was powerfully sweet. He took small bites, surprised that the smooth pulp was warm to the touch. He managed to finish the fruit, knowing his body required nourishment.

"I'll take a swig of water now," David announced, as the fair distribution of supplies was of great concern.

"This is a good time for it. Make sure everyone keeps up with their water needs." Miguel ate his allotted ripened banana. He skipped his share of water once again, promising himself to limit his water intake to a daily evening drink. It took much self control, as the powerful need gnawed restlessly behind every conscious thought. But he couldn't risk David's chances. He'd never be able to face Rosa again. He leaned back to rest, securing the tiller under his arm.

As Toro examined his companions, he grew pleased. He had worried that they would demand vengeance if they learned his identity. But the crew posed little challenge to him. Miguel was tough, protecting everything that ensured his and his son's well being. Yet with all his preparations and leadership, the man was debilitated by sea sickness. He was sparing in his water intake, further weakening his feeble state. If his strength did not reverse soon, someone else would have to take command.

Luis was certainly not the man for it. He needed guidance and survived on approval. For all his fears and blunders, the man was likable. He was like an innocent mongrel puppy.

David had the build of a man, but he had a lot to learn. Of the three, he posed the greatest challenge. He took to heart the protection of the raft, as though it was his domain. Without his *papi*, he would need direction.

Toro was the only one capable of leading them. Too bad the boy hadn't learned to respect him. He could see it in David's eyes. Though Toro could swear David knew nothing of his involvement in butchering the cow, there was a cloud of resentment for him behind the young man's green gaze. Toro lifted up his sombrero and fanned his head. He could handle David's hate.

Miguel rolled onto his stomach and leaned over the side. The little he had managed to consume left his mouth in convulsive spewing. When his stomach stopped contracting, he splashed his face with handfuls of salt water. He was angry at his weakening body. He had taken on a great responsibility by placing his son in such risk. He feared he would not be strong enough to look after him.

"Here, Papi, drink a little water."

Reluctantly, Miguel obeyed. He wanted to stretch the supply of water, not misuse it by throwing it up every time he drank.

"I see the shark's fin! He's far away!" Luis yelled, pointing towards the southern horizon.

With little interest, David's eyes found the dark speck that was causing the man's concern. A shiver of dread froze his tired muscles. "That's no shark fin."

Miguel dug through their belongings and raised the binoculars to his eyes. "It's the Border Guard. No one else would be traveling south of us." Studying the craft for a few moments, he said ominously, "It's a gunboat. A big one. I can make out the white dome of their radar and torpedoes on the side."

"Are we still within Cuban waters?" David asked, hoping the patrol boat would not go any farther.

"I would guess we haven't gone very far," Miguel said, regret marking his tone. "At best, we're moving two miles per hour."

Disdainfully, Toro swatted the air. "These thugs don't respect international law, anyway. If they're after someone, that's not going to slow them down." Toro feared the Border Guard was putting extra effort into this pursuit. Perhaps they had linked his identity with the butchering of the cow by now and knew of his departure when they found the truck. It would appear, from the size of the gunboat, that they were after something more important than pitiful rafters.

Fright covered Luis' face in sweat. "Do you think they're looking for us?"

"Of course they're looking for us!" Toro answered. "Someone probably reported my truck abandoned at the beach."

"We've got you to thank for this, then." David's voice dripped with sarcasm.

"I'm glad to see you're grateful," Toro said, disregarding the intention of David's remark. "If it wasn't for my truck, you might not have launched the raft in time."

"What do you think they'll do to us?" Luis' voice was a trembling whisper.

"I've already been under investigation, thanks to that scoundrel, Tomás Pico," David said with concern. "They'll put me away for two crimes against the state, killing the cow and trying to escape punishment for it. They won't believe in my innocence about the cow this time."

Upon hearing David's angry words, Toro felt a wave of heat rise to his ears. David knew Tomás Pico had been Pepe's partner and believed the street version of the events. Toro would have to be careful hiding his secret. Still, he'd rather take his chances on the raft, and deal with the wrath of the father and son, than be taken back to Cuba.

Miguel didn't dare voice his fears. He knew the danger in store for them was more malevolent than David's concern. He had heard that patrol boat crews destroyed rafts even with people still clinging to them, forcing the drowning men and women to climb into the patrol boat. Their methods included water cannons to dislodge the people and sink the vessel, or heavy sand bags dropped to break apart the flimsy materials that kept them afloat. Often, the sand bags landed on an unfortunate rafter, taking him under along with the remains of the raft. Whether their quarry was taken back for punishment or received his punishment at sea, the guards had accomplished their orders. Miguel couldn't share his apprehension with the others.

"Have they spotted us?" David asked his father.

"I don't know, *hijo*," Miguel said, his eyes glued to the binoculars. "We are pretty low in the water, but in this bright light we are set off against the horizon."

"I'll lower the sail so we give them less of a target to spot." David went to work loosening the ropes.

"We're not an easy mark. Take a look," Toro said with assurance. He swung his chin in the direction of the northwest sky.

David assessed the horizon ahead, as Toro indicated. It was dark and streaked with gray and beige like the mildewed canvas. Rolling the sail into a bundle, David wondered which of the two forces should be considered the enemy and which the savior: the hated Border Guard or the equally threatening storm.

Within endless anxious minutes, the calm crystalline surface of the water was broken by restless peaks. The raft swayed. The weakened men braced themselves against the sides and held on. The soft breeze that had carried them all day, now whipped up into forceful gusts. The men's hair spun and their clothes picked up the wind and flapped. Toro stored his wide-brimmed hat in his canvas sack, then tied the sack to the raft with a rope. The others gathered their supplies and secured them as best they could. Then, Toro helped David store the removable tiller and lift the rudder out of the water.

In the southern distance, the gunboat still traveled in the sunshine, although it was hard to tell in which direction it was headed. But the sun that had mercilessly scorched the men on the raft throughout the day no longer shone on them. A disheartening sense of gloom colored the world that surrounded them. The depth of the restless water now reflected a dark gray. The menacing darkness of the clouds seemed to join the churning seas. Swift shafts of brightness tore through the mounded charcoal skies.

The raft was tossed by the welling seas. Its sides creaked under the stress. Luis cradled his abdomen while holding on with his other hand. His face contorted as a heaving spasm took hold of him. David knew what the man felt, as his head and stomach also swam in a pool of malaise. He worried about his father. Miguel held on, his knuckles turning white from the effort. His eyes were glazed and half shut.

As Toro brought up his knees for better balance, the oars rolled under his legs along the bottom of the raft. Toro went to work tying them up while holding on to the side. David leaned forward and helped with the one-handed task. Toro eyed him curiously. For all his concern about keeping the oars on board, David had neglected to secure them when it really mattered. The boy was not ready for a man's job. Though Toro had to admit that the dread he was sure was building up in their hearts was not surfacing on the boy's face. Only the discomfort of seasickness showed.

Miguel should have been on top of things, but Toro knew the man was too sick to think out plans thoroughly. The color had left their leader's face and he did his best to avoid being tossed out of the raft.

As David searched for the gunboat, a rolling crest broke over the crew. They were drenched before the rainstorm reached them. The sea was an unstable formation of peaks, their foamy tips swept off by the gusts of wind.

"I can't see them anymore," David called out loudly.

When the raft was lifted by a swell, the men craned their necks to scan the seas. The source of their previous anxiety was no longer visible. The raft had been enveloped by the cold gray ferocity of the approaching storm.

"We got away!" Toro raised a fist in celebration.

David shook his head with puzzled disdain. They had entered the cavernous maw of a storm and the man was cheering victory. In spite of the dreadful fate the gunboat had represented, David now felt a vague sense of abandonment. It was as if they had been left by their fellow men to face the raging elements as their penalty.

A bolt of blinding light ripped the skies. The thunderous clap jolted everyone aboard.

"Holy Mother!" Luis screamed.

"I thought you were counting on St. Anthony!" Toro teased him.

Luis scrambled to the back of the raft, suddenly reminded of his plastic guardian. "I can't see it! St. Anthony is gone. He can't desert us!"

"Sit down, Luis!" David ordered. The statue was the least of his worries. "I'm sure it's still attached."

"I can't see it!" Luis kneeled and tugged at the string. He faced the others, distress etched on his brow. "Without him, we're lost!"

"It's still there," Toro yelled. "See? Right in front of the shark." Toro's smile exposed the gap in his teeth.

There was no sign of a gray fin, but the mention was enough to send Luis into spasms of fear. The whites of his eyes circled his dark irises. "Where's the shark?"

"Damn it! Tell him there's no shark," David growled at Toro. Their position was perilous, yet the unpredictable man insisted on having fun at Luis' expense. "This is no time for jokes. Tell him you didn't see a shark."

"I guess my eyes played a trick on me," Toro said unconvincingly, his amused smile never fading.

"There's no shark around here," David said to Luis. "No creature would be foolish enough to enter hell like we have."

A slanting sheet of rain came down on the raft. Water ran down their heads and their drenched clothes. The relentless wind blew across the diminutive vessel. Though the air wasn't cold, they were soon chilled to the core. David tilted his head and allowed the rainwater to fill his mouth. The salt washing down from his face gave the water a slightly salty quality, yet his parched tongue was refreshed.

Bullets of rain shattered the surface of the water, already broken up by heaving peaks. It washed the bottom of the raft and exited through the openings designed to allow excess water to run out.

"Papi, try to catch some rainwater with your mouth," David yelled. The wind blasted their ears and made it difficult for their voices to be heard. He worried about Miguel's weakened state.

In answer, Miguel blinked his eyes.

The raft, with its living cargo, suddenly dipped into a watery trench that formed and spread even as the raft slid into it. The men were lifted and slammed back down onto the wood by the sudden drop. David's stomach seemed to rise to his throat, but there was no time to dwell on it. Just as suddenly, the raft rose again, propelled by a welling hill of water. The wooden vessel was lifted and suspended momentarily, then dropped, as its liquid pedestal receded from under it. The raft slammed down, jarring the forces that held it together.

"Did you count on this when you built it?" David yelled over the roar of the rain.

"I built it strong as I could." Miguel tried to contain the crew's fears, but he knew that the only thing that kept them afloat was the tar-coated foam. He prayed that his work would hold together.

The jute rope that fastened the plastic bottles of drinking water was tightly stretched. The heavy containers jostled against the unstable bottom. In the dimming light, David noticed his father's eyes on the precious cargo.

"I tied them up securely," he assured him loudly, but he worried that the fibers would unravel under the stress.

"No time to think about it now! Just hold on!" A rolling crest of stinging salt water slapped the men. The water forced its way down Miguel's open mouth. He choked. As he gasped for air, David stared, powerless. Miguel coughed up the salt water and panted like a running dog.

The vessel slid down a liquid slope that stretched forever, then suddenly rose. The drenched wind buffeted the crew.

"¡*Aaayyy!*" Luis' scream lasted an eternity.

"Hold on, Papi! We'll make it!"

Toro wouldn't place a bet on that. His tense fists grasped the wooden beam that lined the side. He had never imagined weather this powerful. He bowed to the ferocity of the wind and the sea as he had not bowed to any man. He had scoffed at women's need to pray in hard times and had little patience for Luis' reliance on a statue. Yet he wondered if it was time to turn to a Higher Force for deliverance.

There was no moment of peace. No time to let up on the sore muscles that tightly gripped onto their hope for salvation. They were victims of nature's frenzied carnival ride. Only brute strength and the integrity of the vessel would determine the survivors of this night.

Chapter

7

Torrents of rain hammered at them for hours. The last bit of heat had been drained from David. He shivered uncontrollably. David could hear his father's irregular gasps as he trembled and was relieved he was still on the raft. They were at the edge of exhaustion, he was sure.

Although the raft rocked incessantly, the movement had become regular, less agitated, like a horse-drawn cart ride on uneven cobbles. They were covered in a thick veil of darkness. As the rain diminished to sporadic sprinkles, David brought his hand up and could not make it out in front of his face. In the silence, he wondered if the others had been washed overboard.

"Luis, are you with us?" he asked.

"I'm right across from you," Luis answered in halting syllables, shaking from cold.

David couldn't detect Toro's presence. The man had been such a source of irritation that the thought of his absence brought him peace. He wondered if Toro had been swept away by a wave or if exhaustion had loosened his grip on the raft. David pictured Toro's agonized face gasping for a last breath before the forces of the sea dragged him under. He shuddered. He disliked Toro, but the possibility that he had suffered such a terrible end distressed David.

It didn't escape Toro that David had not called out his name. "Like it or not, I'm here too." Toro waited for a response, but he got none. He chuckled tiredly.

David was relieved. Death was too serious a punishment to wish on the irritating man.

Despite cramps in his muscles, Toro had held on for his life. He was sure the boy wished it wasn't so. The hate David held for him was insignificant compared to the fury of the storm. If he had survived the night, David's hate posed no threat.

Toro groped in the dark for the duffel bag at his side. The knots that lashed it closed were undisturbed. He felt along the length of the canvas, like a doctor palpating a patient's abdomen. He was pleased. There were no rips through which his supplies could have slipped out. Although water dribbled out of the contents, he was satisfied there had been little harm to his necessities for life.

They lay quietly for hours, robbed of strength. David could not find the needed escape of sleep. He wondered where the storm had taken them. Were they closer to Florida, now or had they been dragged far north? They would drift with the northeast flow of the Gulf Stream to the safety of Florida. But, if the storm had taken them too far north, where the Gulf Stream's course moves away from the coast, its grip would carry the raft away from land. David shut his eyes tightly. They had no way of knowing their position.

A third sunrise greeted the floating passengers. It was ironic that the sun's rays touched them with such energy. The men were drained of power. Miguel lay unmoving. The lids that covered his eyes were puffy. Dark half moons lined his lower lashes.

For once, the warmth carried welcome renewal. As his body absorbed the heat, David's shivering limbs relaxed. But taking stock of his surroundings, he sat up horrified.

"The water jugs! They're gone!" he screamed, greatly distressed. "Papi, the rope broke apart and the bottles were washed over!"

Miguel opened his eyes weakly. "Are they all gone?"

"All but two gallons. I had tied them separately." David knew they'd need more than that to survive. "It's that worthless jute! It couldn't hold up to the rough treatment. It was old and worn out from the start."

"I'm sorry. I wish I'd found better rope." Luis leaned forward to pat David's shoulder. David jerked back.

He knew Luis wasn't to blame. The items they had listed for the trip had been very difficult to come by. The search had to be done on the sly. He and Miguel had accepted what Luis had brought to them. But the blame for David's desperation had to lay on someone.

"We'll make it. You'll see, *hermano*," Luis said with remorse, calling him brother. "We'll share our water. I've got a half gallon left."

Toro wrapped a protective leg over his canvas duffel.

David took a deep angry breath. Luis' portion of water was less per man than he and his father had. They would have to cut their supply to help Luis. Yet, in his dim reasoning, Luis thought he was helping them.

"Is that all you brought?" David shook his head angrily.

"One gallon. But I drank some of it."

Luis' nature was so simple, David could not vent his wrath on him. Anger turned into hopelessness. Luis had called him brother. The familial connection didn't exist, but David knew the man was right. They were all brothers in misfortune. The same fate awaited them, whether they reached safety or died. They would all go together.

David studied the items lashed to the wood beams. As his eyes rested on Toro's bag, Toro jumped up defensively.

"Don't get any ideas. The things in here are for my survival." He wasn't willing to share. At least not yet, no one was in desperate need. Let David learn to fend for himself.

"I didn't say a word, hothead!"

Toro smiled—David could be so easily riled.

On hands and knees, David looked for the sack of food they had stashed by his father. It wasn't where they had secured it just before the storm. David reached carefully behind Miguel, feeling only the rolled up canvas of the sail. In a panic, he looked around. The bag was gone. Gone also were the soft bananas, the peanuts, the raisins and Rosa's precious gift of condensed milk and juice that were inside the bag.

The small tackle box with their fishing gear had also disappeared. There was nothing David could do to replace the devastating loss of their food and drink. He could not burden his spent father with the horrible news.

David's body dropped heavily back where he had been sitting. He sank into despair. They had no food and very little water. They must reach safety soon, it was their only hope. He remembered the promise his mother had drawn from him. David did not consider himself a religious person, but he knelt down and patted his father's pockets until he found the small statue of the Virgin. Without removing it from Miguel's pants, he took a breath of relief.

David had always looked for ways to solve his own problems, but now he didn't know what he could do. Perhaps it was time to keep his promise to his mother.

Without consulting anyone, Toro stood up and tested the strength of the mast. Bending down, he put an arm around Miguel to lift him.

"Get your hands off my father!" David warned.

Toro ignored him and pulled the canvas sail free of the weight of the man. David shrank back, ashamed. Toro was setting up the sail. David should have thought to harness the wind.

"That end goes up," David instructed, spreading his legs apart as he stood to help.

"Sit down! You're going to capsize us," Toro said harshly. "Set up the rudder and tiller and guide us northwest."

David did as Toro said. He was unhappy, to have to follow orders from the man, but he had to admit that Toro's reasoning was sound. They would have to work for their salvation.

Luis was eagerly studying the ripples behind the raft. "What did I tell you?" he yelled excitedly, then answered his own question. "I said we'd make it!"

David and Toro looked where he pointed with anticipation. Toro squinted to better scan the horizon for a ship. He had heard of many rafters being rescued by merchant ships. This could be their opportunity.

"Where do you see it?" Toro asked. Standing in the center of the small vessel, he had a good vantage point, yet he couldn't detect anything significant.

"There," Luis pointed behind them with a happy grin.

Eagerly, David loosened the binoculars secured by their strap to a beam. He strained to look through them. But all he saw was broken glass and puddled water. "¡*Caramba*! The stupid thing cracked in the storm!" Angrily, he threw the useless instrument in the water. The splash a few yards away startled Luis.

"What was that?" he asked shakily.

"Nothing that can harm you," David said with a smile, hopeful about the new turn in their fortune. Anxious to make out the ship, he asked, "Where is it? I want to see it!"

"Right there! See?" Luis said pointing to the spray a few yards behind them. "St. Anthony's still attached to the string."

David's spirits sagged. His hope dimmed.

"¡*Idiota*!" Toro yelled, fuming. He shoved Luis against the side and grabbed the collar of his shirt. "We thought you had seen a ship! Don't do that again! Who cares about your saint?"

"Don't talk that way," Luis said, raising his eyes to the heavens. "I don't want him to turn his back on us."

"Forget it!" Toro said, releasing him so that the man dropped heavily against the boards.

David set course with the help of the morning sun. The rudder had not suffered harm and he welcomed the lucky discovery after the morning's string of misfortunes.

"Hold the tiller for a moment," he told Luis.

When they traded places, David knelt by Miguel. "Papi, I want you to drink some water." He went to work carefully measuring a few drops into a tin cup that had survived the night. He lifted his father's head onto his lap and brought the cup to his swollen cracked lips. Miguel didn't open his eyes, but when the drops touched his mouth, his tongue maneuvered the water down his throat.

When David felt he had given him a suitable amount, he lowered Miguel's head to the bottom of the raft.

Miguel's hand weakly took hold of his son's wrist, anticipating he would move away. He pulled him down close to him. "*Hijo*," he whispered. "When you reach Miami, call Gabriel."

"*Sí*, Papi."

"His number is in my pocket, with my other papers." Miguel's voice was raspy. Swollen, discolored lids covered his eyes.

A cold fear invaded David. Miguel seemed to be preparing him to handle things alone. David couldn't accept that. His father was weakened by seasickness and the stress of the storm. But it wasn't anything they couldn't overcome...if their water lasted, of course.

"Papi, *you* will call him. You'll see Gabriel when we get to Florida."

Miguel shook his head weakly. "Get your mother and sister out of Cuba. Never give up, never forget."

"Papi, we'll do it together, you and I."

"Promise me," Miguel's voice was soft and slow, but deliberate. "Promise you'll send your mother a pair of leather shoes. Like the ones she traded for our sake."

David couldn't quite remember the style of the shoes, but this was no time to tell his father that. He nodded his head. "*Sí*, Papi. I promise."

Unbuttoning his shirt, David took out the cap from its safe storage, flattened against his belly and placed it over Miguel's face.

"Sleep, Papi. I'll take care of things."

Toro shook his head. As he examined Miguel's prone body, he could tell the man was not giving in to normal sleep. Toro did nothing to interfere with David's illusion.

Elena waited anxious moments after knocking on the door of the Leal home. She twirled a handkerchief nervously around her fingers. She had been frightfully worried. After three days she had worked up enough courage to approach Rosa. Elena wondered how David's mother would react when she learned Elena knew about the men's journey. The men's escape from the country left the family vulnerable to accusations of antisocial acts. Rosa might be wary even of a young girl.

Rosa's brow tensed when she saw Elena at the door. "*Sí*, Elena. What is it?" Rosa's voice had little life.

Elena could see that Rosa was distressed, her eyes were rimmed with red and her short hair was uncombed. Elena drew close to the woman and whispered, "I came to ask about David."

The girl hadn't seen her *novio*, her young sweetheart, for a few days and missed him, Rosa reasoned. Still, Rosa eyed her with suspicion. It was difficult to trust anyone. "He's fine," Rosa answered loudly to make herself heard by distrustful neighbors. "He went with his father to the countryside."

Elena was taken back by the woman's answer. "Have you heard from him?"

"No, I haven't. They wanted to check out the agrarian school," Rosa lied. She hated to carry on her charade, but she couldn't be sure of the girl. She had to protect Diana and herself.

Elena's brow furrowed. With a tremor to her lips, Elena confided, "I know where they went." Elena's eyes were serious as she returned Rosa's gaze.

"Then you know they'll be back soon." Rosa was defiant. She wondered if Elena's words were meant as a threat. If word got out that her husband and son had left the country, the family's ration book could be confiscated and she wouldn't be allowed to work. Rosa started to push the door closed. "I'm very busy. I have to get back to my housework."

"Mrs. Leal," Elena's voice cracked with emotion. "You and I know they're not returning. I was there when they 'jumped off' at the cove."

A mixture of hope and panic twisted Rosa's heart. "Come into the house," Rosa invited the girl nervously.

In hushed tones, Elena described how the men put the raft in the water and shoved off. She told Rosa about the abandoned government truck.

"I went back the next morning because I couldn't believe it had really happened. When I saw the waves splashing on the truck, I knew I hadn't dreamed it all up." Elena swallowed hard. "Then, the police found the truck and I hid."

"Why didn't you tell me about this sooner?" Rosa was filled with disturbing thoughts.

"I wanted to come to you right away. I couldn't share what I knew with anyone else." Rosa drew a sigh of relief. The girl hadn't told anyone. "But I was

133

afraid you'd be suspicious of me," Elena said, tears welling in her eyes.

"I'm sorry, Elena," Rosa said. "Our way of life makes you distrust your own blood at times." Rosa paced the floor trying to figure things out. "I'm sure the police notified the Border Guard."

"Do you think they were captured?"

"It seems word would have gotten to me somehow." Even while reassuring Elena, Rosa had trouble concealing her alarm. Her husband and son could be in jail. Or they could have been killed at sea by the guards. Rosa shuddered.

"Did they have enough food and water for four?" Elena asked with concern.

"There were only three on the raft," Rosa corrected her.

"No. Four men left on the raft," Elena said firmly. "The man who drove the truck 'jumped off' with them. I could hear them arguing. I suppose the others didn't want him along."

Rosa worried about this new problem. They had an unwelcome passenger on the small raft. "If he didn't bring supplies for himself, they won't make it. They barely had enough for three."

Trails of tears streaked Elena's face. Her voice quivered. "How long does it take to get to Florida?"

Rosa shook her head. "It depends." She took a labored breath to harness her emotions. "I'll call Miami right away."

It was late afternoon by the position of the sun when Toro spotted a large object in the water. "Look over to the north," he alerted David.

"What do you make of it?" David asked as his eyes examined the floating form.

Luis awakened from a light slumber. He strained to see what the others were discussing. Miguel lay motionless.

"Looks like a strange boat. Maybe it's another raft." Luis craned his neck to look and Toro teased him. "Don't worry, Luis. Whatever it is, it's not alive!"

"I'll set course for it," David said, turning the tiller a few degrees.

Toro and Luis set their oars in place and rowed. They were anxious and didn't want to wait for the gentle breeze to do its slow work.

The sight that greeted the men sobered them. A wood frame enclosed several truck inner tubes wrapped in canvas and other fabrics. Gaps in the assorted pieces of lumber revealed the limp condition of most of the rubber inner tubes. The flat part of the craft, which at one time must have held the passengers, slanted into the water. There was no one on board.

The hairs on David's neck rose and prickled. The fellow rafters must have perished. The loose boards and dangling canvas made him keenly aware of how close they had come to suffering a similar fate. "Do you suppose they were washed out in last night's storm?"

A reverent hush came over the men.

"Looks like it." Toro flinched with uneasiness.

"You think they drowned?" Luis asked unwilling to accept such an end. "Maybe they were rescued."

David shook his head somberly.

"Let's check it out," Toro suggested. "Maybe there's provisions or something useful tucked away in the wreck. The owners don't have any use for the stuff now."

The cold way Toro put it chilled David. But he realized what Toro said was right. If the missing rafters had left something behind that could save them, their loss would have some significance.

Maneuvering close to the sinking raft, Toro took his oar out of the water. He leaned over and grabbed a loose rope trailing from the abandoned raft. "I've got a hold of it," he said, then motioned to David. "Hop into it and see if there's anything we can use."

"Why me?" David asked suspiciously.

Toro looked him in the eye. "I can't trust Luis to tie his shoe laces right. How could he handle a job like this?"

"You do it, then," David proposed.

"I'm the only one left with the strength to hold the rope and keep the rafts together. Looks to me like you're the best man for the job."

David knew he was right. He was feeling very tired. He couldn't remember the last time he had eaten anything. Besides, their provisions were so low they couldn't pass up a chance like this. "Get the two rafts side by side," David told Toro.

Luis' mouth was wide open, frozen by the excitement and danger of what was about to take place.

Toro wrapped the fraying rope around the stake that served as an oarlock and pulled. He aligned the homemade vessels. "That's as close as I can get them. I don't want those timbers to rub against the dense packing foam that's keeping us afloat."

"I'll give it a try," David agreed. Looking down at the gap of deep blue water that separated the two floating objects, David gulped down a breath of courage. Although he knew how to swim, he didn't like the thought of doing it so far from land.

David waited for synchrony in the sway of the rafts, which took place randomly for a split moment every few minutes. Then, he jumped.

Luis watched in awe, his eyes like white saucers sparkling with the light of fear. His mouth was a gaping cave.

David stumbled forward, landing on the tilted, flooded floor. His clothes were soaked. But he was unhurt, floating above the water in the questionable safety of the deteriorating craft. He didn't waste any time to look around in the recessed areas where the boards met. His hands shook as he felt around.

"Anything there?" Toro asked.

"I found a towel in a plastic bag."

"A lot of good that will do us," Toro said dejectedly.

David put the bag in the waistband of his pants. "I found something! It's a canteen with liquid in it. Only half full," David reported. He unscrewed the cap and took a swig. "It's water!"

"Hand it over!"

David threw it across into Toro's hands, suddenly feeling vulnerable without it. He had given little thought to the position he was in until now. Toro controlled David's survival. The thought crossed his mind that this could have been Toro's ploy to get him off the raft. Without him and with his father so weak, Toro would have full charge. The fewer the men, the farther the meager supplies would extend. David wondered if the man was capable of such betrayal.

As Toro examined the military style canteen, the rope holding the rafts together slipped and the distance between the rafts widened.

The breeze had filled the sail and the raft was moving away from the disabled vessel, David noticed with shock. "Lower the sail! The raft's moving away!" he yelled, anxiety and anger coloring his voice.

Toro rushed to take apart the knots that secured the sail. His fingers worked fast, but not fast enough to prevent the wind from giving the raft a final shove.

"You're losing the rope!" David shouted. He wondered if Toro's efforts to help him would be sincere. He shuddered to think he'd be abandoned in the sinking craft.

"Don't just stand there! Grab the rope!" Toro yelled at Luis.

Breaking his spell as enthralled observer, Luis quickly leaned over. The frayed tip of the swiftly slipping rope caressed his fingers and the end of the rope sank. His eyes followed the rope into the depths. Then, Luis saw the familiar dreaded predator, darting with curiosity around the sinking end of rope.

"¡*Tiburón!*" He pulled away from the side in panic. "There's two or three of them! Don't fall in! They're under your raft!" Luis' voice was shrill with fear of his discovery.

Toro looked down into the water, his hands working fast to lower the sail. As he confirmed Luis' fearful words, Toro's lips compressed and his nostrils flared in exasperation.

Squatting in a puddle of water, David peered through the wide gaps on the raft floor. He felt the blood drain from his face. Three swift predators aimlessly followed an evil dance. David tried to do something useful to get his racing mind on a steady course again. He grabbed the end of the rope that was secured to the wooden frame. He pulled it out of the ocean, keeping a wary eye on the sharks that followed it.

"Take hold of your oar and start paddling," Toro commanded Luis.

Toro and Luis sat on the rowing seat, gripped the oars firmly and pulled on the water with short repetitive strokes. If they were making progress towards David, they couldn't tell.

"He's coming after it!" Luis shouted, jerking the business end of the oar out of the water. "He's attacking my oar!"

"Keep paddling! The shark can't hurt the oar!" Toro said.

Luis gingerly tried again. With shaky hands, he placed the oar in the water and pushed. The shark made a pass at the oar again and he pulled it out. "He's back!"

"I can't paddle alone! If you keep this up, we'll get further away!" Toro said disgusted with the man. They had to work carefully and fast.

When Luis eyed the water with caution but didn't make a move to paddle, Toro swatted him. "Get moving!"

Luis did as told. The furious pace of his strokes reflected his panic. As they got closer to David, a sleek gray form shot out under the surface, attracted by the thrashing movement of Luis' oar.

"He tried to bite my oar! He's coming for me!" Luis slapped the water with the oar, sending a wing of spray onto himself and Toro. Provoked, the shark returned.

Attracted by the erratic commotion which was similar to that of an injured fish, his companions dashed to the surface. Passing under the board that supported David, a sleek shark rubbed against the wood. David winced. Estimating by the length of the board, the shark measured eight feet. David's knuckles whitened as he gripped the wreck for his life.

As the trio of curious beasts darted around the red wooden oar, Luis shook with fear.

"Stop splashing. You're driving them crazy!" David yelled.

"Get your oar out of the water!" Toro shouted.

Luis pulled the dripping oar into the raft. The color had drained from his dark face.

Toro plunged his oar into the water cautiously. Toro respected the sharks, but he didn't want to give the men the impression he feared them. He drew the red oar through the water. A shark approached it to investigate. With deliberate measured strokes, Toro paddled with all his strength. The other men watched apprehensively. In a few minutes, the rafts drew closer.

"Throw the rope over," Toro said, laying down the oar with care.

David knelt in the puddle. Through the slits in the boards, he saw a gray sleek form dart under him. He wouldn't let his fears drain him of power. He braced himself against a board, then swung the coil of rope over his head. When Toro caught it and pulled, David drew a sigh of relief.

"Easy," Toro said as he pulled the disabled vessel toward the raft. "I'll bring them as close as I dare to."

The wreck and its unfortunate passenger glided silently across. Toro's hands burned from the strain.

"Grab the timbers and keep them from rubbing against our raft," Toro instructed Luis. Luis reached above the water, fear etched in his dark eyes. His trembling hands made contact with the jutting beams and he held on.

"Make room for me," David said, cautiously clambering to a standing position. Then with his heart in his throat, he leaped safely into his father's raft.

Chapter

8

Rosa rushed to her neighbor's house when she was told a telephone connection to Miami had been reached. She had known Alba González for many years. But despite all the years they had lived on the same street, Rosa could not risk telling her why she was using her telephone. She did not know Alba's true feelings about the government. Some people derived great satisfaction and prestige in the eyes of the police for turning in lawbreakers. In the wrong hands, the reason for her call could bring on punishment.

Diana, who was playing in a friend's yard, saw Rosa and joined her.

"Diana, I want you to go back to Magy's house. I'll be right back."

"I want to go with you" Diana insisted.

Although Rosa didn't want Diana involved in this, she had no time to spare. Besides, she had too much on her mind to argue. She had to make a desperate request for help. So much depended on it. Yet, she had to code her message to Gabriel. It was like speaking a foreign language and never slipping into your native tongue for fear of punishment.

Alba González waited by the door to her house. "Quick, we've got the operator waiting for you."

"*¡Hola! Sí, es Rosa Leal,*" Rosa identified herself to the operator. Her face suddenly brightened. "Gabriel! How good it is to hear your voice." She paused and then nodded as if the person at the end of the line could see her. "Yes, I did. My operation went through three days ago."

Diana's jaw dropped open. Her mother hadn't been to the hospital; she hadn't even been sick.

"There were some complications. Another doctor insisted on helping. In all there were four doctors in the operating room." Rosa had to make Gabriel understand there were four men on the raft, as they might be out of drinking water by now.

Diana cocked her head, puzzled.

"No, I'm not feeling well. I think I may have an infection, although I don't know what kind." Rosa's voice cracked. Tears gathered in the corners of her eyes. Infection was their code word for danger.

Diana worried about her mother. Rosa seemed deeply affected by her condition. And she had kept it all from her.

"Yes, send the best medicine you can find. Lots of it." Rosa's mouth trembled and her words were filled with anguish. She hoped Gabriel would ask the pilots at Brothers to the Rescue to look for

Miguel's raft. "I'm very grateful, Gabriel. Yes I'll take care of myself. *Adiós*, Goodbye." She wanted to ask him to call her as soon as he knew anything about David and Miguel, but she couldn't figure out how to put it in code. She trusted Gabriel would do that without being reminded.

As she put down the receiver, she noticed her hand shook.

"Here's a little coffee." Alba offered her a tiny cup of the potent Cuban drink. "It will make you feel stronger. You're holding up pretty well after such a big operation."

Rosa's skin prickled with distrust. She knew her appearance and movements were not those of someone who was sick. As Rosa took the cup, Alba winked her eye as though conspiring with her. Anxious to leave now, Rosa drank the coffee quickly.

The look of shock on Diana's face reminded Rosa she must take the girl home. She had to tell her the truth in privacy. She must leave before Diana asked any questions that would give Rosa away.

"Thank you for letting me use the telephone. I must be going now," she said, grabbing Diana's arm and leading her out.

Alba walked her to the door. She put her hand on Rosa's shoulder. "I know what you're feeling," she said holding Rosa's gaze with hers. "Many of us would like to have the same operation. We are all feeling just as sick."

There was no mistaking the meaning of her words. Still cautious, Rosa knew she had found a friend.

~~~~~~~

Toro worried about how fast their provisions had disappeared. But seeing the condition of the listless crew, he knew he couldn't eat what little he had without offering them some. David and Luis had not eaten much all day. Their food was all gone. The exertion devoted to the discovery of the sinking raft had worn them further down.

"I've got some crackers left. Take one each. We'll have to make them stretch." Toro held out the bag. "This is the end of our food."

David was surprised at Toro's generous move. He noticed he had referred to his cache of food as the group's supplies.

Ravenously, Luis grabbed a cracker. His fever-ish eyes were grateful. "*Gracias, hermano.*"

Toro shoved the bag at David, who stared at the food, yet hesitated. Pride shone in David's eyes, but his hunger had the upper hand. David reached in, took a cracker and, looking Toro squarely in the eye, nodded his thanks.

David savored each bite and took his last drink of the day. Then, as he had done each time they had allotted refreshment for themselves, David looked after his weak father.

"Papi, here's some water for you." David held his father's head up in the dimming light. Miguel's eyes were closed. A few of the precious drops dribbled out of his mouth and David scooped them up with the tin cup. "Come on, Papi. We'll soon be there. You've got to drink some water." Miguel didn't answer, but his tongue accepted the measured drink.

The burnt skin on Miguel's forehead lifted up in long dry flakes. The tender layer underneath looked raw. David rubbed his own forehead, wondering if his skin was peeling too. He winced at the touch of his own hand on the crusty, painful flesh.

As the sun set, a feeling of gloom overtook the men on the raft. They were sure the sharks that had keenly awakened the men's respect were keeping up with the strange craft. The blinding darkness, which made water and sky indistinct, served to build up the men's insecurity. David's imagination conceived of terrors that he knew to be impossible in reality. He feared that if he gave in to sleep, a shark would surely know it and take advantage of the moment.

Luis had begun to confuse reality with the pictures in his mind. Since his run-in with the beasts, he had hollered threats to them and moaned with dread that the sharks would not obey him. David and Toro had tried to calm his fears, but the man believed he could achieve some control over the sharks. He had fallen into a restless sleep, gurgling commands at the enemy.

Sometime during the endless night, David felt a movement at his left side. With the acute ability of prey in danger, he became fully awakened. His father lay to his left. But he was sure it had not been his father's movement he had felt. He heard short grunts, the type someone would make who was expending much effort. On his right, Luis snored. It could only be Toro at Miguel's side. David's blood raced with alarm. He had allowed Toro's cooperation and generosity to blind him to the man's ugly nature. David felt betrayed. Toro was taking advantage of his father's weakened state. He was robbing him!

"Get your dirty hands off my father!" David jumped onto and wrestled the dark figure. "*¡Descarado!* You're stealing his watch!"

"Take it easy!" Toro warned. He was surprised by the sudden attack. "I've got a knife in my hand!"

"I've had enough of your threats!" David yelled, shoving the man away from Miguel. "You don't scare me with your weapon! I should throw you in the water and let the sharks have what they've been after!"

At the other side of the raft, Luis gasped loudly.

Toro snorted in anger. He had warned David about the knife to avoid hurting someone or dropping it into the water. He hadn't meant it as a threat.

"I should have pushed you off back at the cove." David forced his words through his clenched teeth. His hands gripped Toro's arms forcefully. "You wouldn't have had the guts to call the Border Guard on us. You were too involved in our plans."

The small raft had become the center of a wrestling match. The two were locked in a bitter embrace. The raft rocked.

"If you give me a minute..."

"I'm not giving you anything!" David cut Toro off. "I don't trust a single hair on your head! For all I know, you took our water and food during the storm and put it in that duffel bag of yours!"

Toro was indignant. He shoved David back. "Go check the bag! You'll find nothing in it but what I brought from home!"

"I'm not falling for that! I'm not about to let go of you to look in the bag!"

"I didn't take anything from you!" Toro said angrily. He'd had enough! His help had been mistaken for robbery. "And I'm not stealing from Miguel now! I have more self respect than to steal from a man who's barely breathing!" Toro paused, took a slow breath, then continued calmly. "I'm cutting rope to tie him up."

David felt his blood boil. Toro had admitted his dirty deed! He swatted Toro away from his father. "I suppose, after my father is out of the way, you plan to tie up Luis and me too. That's if we ever sleep with both eyes closed!"

"¡*Qué estúpido eres!*" Toro said with disgust. He retreated to his side of the raft, giving up his attempt to help. "You are a stupid little boy! You're too blinded by duty to see that your father is unconscious!"

David shook his head in disbelief, gazing down at Miguel. In the shifting light of dawn, he could now make out his father's outline. "He's just weak. He's been sleeping a lot."

"Not anymore. Talk to him. Ask him to wake up."

David could not revive his father. If Miguel had not awakened to the struggle over his prone body, his son's soft calls would not make him rise. David felt a tremendous weight drop on his shoulders as he accepted the truth of his father's condition. Miguel needed help right away. All David had for him was water. And not much of that.

"He's been drifting away slowly," Toro said quietly. "I've seen it coming. He skipped his rations of water, probably to stretch the supply for you."

David leaned back against the side, spent by the struggle and overcome by stark reality. He no longer could count on his father for advice. On the contrary, his father's survival depended solely on him. From now on, it was a fight against time.

He had misjudged Toro's action. He couldn't bring his eyes up to look at the man. Maybe there was more to Toro than bullying and posturing.

"The wind picked up early this morning. The sea is choppy," Toro said. "We should tie him to the beams so he doesn't get washed off."

David agreed without a word. On their hands and knees, they used a length of rope to secure Miguel to the frame of the raft. As they lifted Miguel's limp body to pass the rope under him, a quick ray of light reflected off something metallic. It caught David's eye. He reached for the object and his heart surged with hope.

"Our crackers! This is our tin of crackers. I thought it was lost in the storm, but it was wedged between the boards behind my father."

"Are they still dry?" Toro asked.

"Listen for yourself!" David laughed as he shook the metal box like a rattle. He pulled up the lid carefully. "They're as fresh as when we took off! Have one," he offered Toro and Luis.

"Take it slow," Toro warned the giddy young man. "These have to last as long as it takes."

"We've had so much go wrong. We owe this to ourselves: a cracker and a sip of water for breakfast." He chuckled bitterly. David knew there was little else to feel good about.

Toro accepted a cracker. "Give your father a drink of my water," he said, handing him a tin cup. "There's sugar in it. It will do him good."

David dribbled a thin stream into Miguel's mouth, surprised at Toro's generosity. The sugar in his water explained how Toro had been fresh while the others had drooped. It had energized him. David was sorry they had not thought to do this.

As he carefully took a measured swig of the precious sweet drink, Toro realized he had emptied one of his water jugs. He was down to one. He wondered how much longer the journey would take. He had never experienced such demanding thirst. It was difficult to overpower this need and ration what he had left.

"Look at the bright side," he told David without enthusiasm. "We are all alive."

After adjusting their course by the rising sun, the men sat tiredly in the warm breeze.

"If we're anywhere near land, this wind will get us there faster," Toro suggested, although his confidence wavered.

"Let's hope so." David raised his brows and quirked his mouth, unsure of their expectations.

"I wonder where the storm took us? It's so hard not to know where you are."

David agreed. Not knowing their location made him feel helpless. For days, they had been floating in a vast sea with little sense of direction, save for the sun and the north star at night. Yet these indicators only showed direction, not location.

"Do you think the airplanes from 'Brothers to the Rescue' fly in weather like this?" Toro looked up at the cloudless sky. Briefly, Luis took his eyes from the trailing statue and glanced up.

"I think they would. It's not that windy," David said, not bothering to scan the skies. "All we ever see are the streaks that the big jets leave across the sky. At that altitude, there's no way anyone can see us."

"Yeah, I sometimes wonder what delicacies are being served to the passengers flying over our heads." Toro rubbed his belly, then bitterly said, "They're sitting in comfort while we..."

"That's enough!" David interrupted. "There's no use thinking about those things. We'll drive ourselves crazy!"

Their eyes went to Luis, who mumbled a vicious threat to unseen enemies under the surface.

"Very well," Toro gave in with a teasing smile. "Let's talk about something we both like. Tell me about that pretty little thing you left at the cove."

A pang of sorrow twisted in David's chest. He missed Elena. He missed the security of her loving attention. But he wouldn't spoil the nice memories by sharing them with Toro. Despite the man having become more cooperative lately, there were things

David would not share with him. David squinted his eyes and shook his head in answer.

Toro tilted his head back and roared with laughter. He knew how to get to David. It felt good to vent his hopelessness with a cleansing laugh.

Annoyed, David got up from his seat to stretch. He held on to the mast and made a big deal of inspecting the condition of the sail. He was pleased that his careful stitches were holding up well. His mother would be proud of how well he had followed her sewing instructions. How would she feel though, if she learned that her husband lay unconscious at David's feet? He brushed away the painful thought.

As his fingers tested the line of stitches along the vertical edge of the sail, David's eyes were suddenly riveted on the horizon. David shook with excitement before the words left his mouth.

"A ship! There's a ship to the west!"

Toro jumped to attention. The large brim of his *sombrero* shielded his eyes from the harsh sun. A joyful smile curved his dry lips. "There she is! She's a beauty. Her outline is as beautiful as a pretty girl's curves."

David couldn't help smiling at the comparison. The ship certainly gave him as much joy and security as Elena...maybe more, in their present dire situation.

"I never dreamed I'd be staring at a far away shadow with such happiness!" Toro exclaimed.

"She is quite far away. We are nothing but a speck in the ocean. They can't see us yet," David pointed out, an edge of caution holding back his joy.

"But she's heading this way," Toro said without a tinge of doubt to his voice. "I can tell by the angle of her shape."

The men watched fascinated, wild thoughts of rescue rushing through their minds.

David's heart thundered in his chest. He gave in to happy anticipation. In his head, he listed his immediate needs, although he couldn't select which one he would satisfy first. He wanted water, a large bucket of the sweet stuff. He'd get food to subdue the constant aching of his empty gurgling stomach. He'd have a soft bed, one that didn't rock endlessly, breaking his uncomfortable sleep. His father would get help… They'd know what to do to get him back to his old self.

"I can't wait to empty a cold bottle of soda into my mouth. I've heard they've got plenty of it on these ships," Toro said licking his dry lips. His lids drooped and his dark eyes had a dreamy glaze. "I remember the sweet bubbly taste like it was yesterday. A friend shared some with me once. He'd gotten it from a grateful foreigner who had shopped at the tourist store."

"I'll be happy with a tub of water. I'll dunk my head into the sweet liquid and lap it up 'til it's empty!" David laughed.

"Tonight, I'll sleep like a baby." Toro's smile exposed all his teeth. "Nothing will disturb me, even if they force me to share a bunk with Luis. I'll hug him like he was a soft pillow!"

David giggled like a little boy.

Their gloom had reversed. They were light-hearted, full of hope. The feeling had rubbed off on Luis, even in his confusion. His dark face was radiant, like an innocent child who is happy for others' joy.

"I'm going to eat and drink until my belly explodes," Luis said, his dark brown hair flying in the breeze.

David smiled. "Can you make out what kind of ship it is?" he asked, as the shape took on a more definite form.

"It looks like a cargo ship," Toro said, unsure. Then, a fearsome thought clouded his joy. "What if the ship is headed for Cuba?"

David's face lost color under the burnt patches. "It's coming from the west. The only land to the west is the United States. They don't trade with Cuba." What he said was true, but he couldn't bring a ring of conviction to his voice. He glanced at Toro for reassurance.

Toro shook his head slowly, also uncertain.

Luis, who had been gleefully sitting in his appointed spot, jumped up suddenly "¡*Ayuda*! ¡*Socorro*!" He screamed for help.

"Save your breath until they're closer. They still can't hear us."

"¡*Ayuda*! ¡*Socorro*!" Luis didn't hear Toro. He was in his own world.

"We need something to draw their attention," said David, watching the desperate man vainly wasting his little energy.

"Let's take off our shirts and wave them over our heads," Toro suggested.

When Toro undressed to the waist and waved his ragged shirt, Luis did the same, imitating the action like a mindless monkey.

David groped between the boards, where he had stashed the tin of crackers. He lifted the lid and carried it to the prow of the tiny craft. Carefully, he captured the sun's rays and reflected them back toward the large ship.

"¡*Vaya*! Hey! At least one of us is using his brains!" Toro praised David.

They waved and signaled for endless minutes, trying to gauge if their desperate efforts had been perceived.

"It's a merchant ship. I can see the rectangular containers stacked up on her." Toro's voice vibrated with excitement.

"Can you tell the ship's nationality?" David asked with apprehension.

"It's hard to make out the flag. But there's writing on the side." Toro squinted under the brim of his straw hat for a better view.

"I see the writing too, but I can't read her name. I can only make out a few of the letters." David stared at the ship intently, as if he could capture its attention with his fierce gaze.

"They're close enough to see us. Keep signaling," Toro said anxiously. But David had not let up on his job.

"Do you think they've altered their course?" David asked, fearing that as the ship approached, its path was taking it north of the tiny raft.

Toro didn't answer. The smile was fading from his face.

"¡*Ayuda!*" Luis screamed, uselessly. "I can see people! They're looking this way!" Luis told the others in his frenzy.

David and Toro strained to see what Luis was sure he spotted. Luis floundered between reality and images in his mind. They didn't rely on his observations anymore.

"I do see them," Toro whispered, his voice tainted with bitterness. He gave David a meaningful side-glance.

David's blood chilled. The tiny shapes of several crewmen stood behind a railing facing in the direction of the raft.

"I hope they get to hell instead of their next port!" Toro cursed between his teeth. A hiss escaped through the gap of his missing eye tooth.

There was no mistaking it. The crew had seen them.

"I had heard of ships passing up stranded rafters, but I didn't believe anyone could be so cold blooded," David said, robbed of enthusiasm.

"They claim it's too inconvenient," Toro said in anger. "They have to wait in port and stick to the government's procedures when they rescue rafters."

"How can they live with themselves? They're ignoring people stranded out here." David did not expect an answer. He doubted anyone knew. He slumped back. He was glad that his father had not been buoyed with hope only to have his desperate wishes dashed.

"¡Ayuda! ¡Socorro!" Luis yelled, frightened as the ship passed them by on its eastern course.

"Give it up! ¡Idiota!" Toro yelled. His eyes were on fire.

Luis stared at Toro, his mouth open. The look on his face showed his incomprehension.

"It's not his fault," David said resignedly. "Don't take it out on him."

Toro slumped down to his seat, his face covered by tense sunburned hands. His thoughts seethed in pools of anger and bitterness. If he could climb onto the passing ship, he'd tow its crew behind it on the raft to give them a taste of misery! He had never felt so dependent, so powerless. How much longer would they float aimlessly—at the mercy of the forces of nature?

David felt an oppressive gloom drift over him as he watched the speck recede further into the horizon. The feeling was as strong as the burning power of the brutal morning sun. Its heat had damaged their skin and sucked the moisture from their bodies. They had suffered debilitating sickness from the constant movement. The storm and endless days at sea had robbed them of their supplies. They were near exhaustion from weakness and lack of sleep. Sharks kept alive their most basic raw fear. The rafters' floating world was restricted and full of menace. And now abandoned by their fellow human beings, David felt complete despair.

It was not David's nature to give up, however. Giving up now meant submitting to a tragic end too early in his life, and David was not ready to accept death. He had to do something! He had to alter the course of their apparent destiny!

Without his father for guidance, David reasoned he had to be responsible not only for himself and for his father's safety, but for the raft and the others.

Luis was no longer able to care for himself, much less be relied upon by the others. David knew he'd have to look out for him, too. If he left Luis to fend for himself, he'd sink as low as the callous crew on the ship.

Toro was beginning to show signs of wear. Still, he seemed to have a larger reserve of energy than any of the others. There were moments when Toro had shown concern and cooperation. Perhaps the reality of their predicament was softening him up. David would have to count on Toro's help and deal with his actions as they came.

Assuming Miguel's role, David considered the steps he needed to take. He'd have to ensure that their course was accurate, even in the night. He would not neglect this duty. Every bit of progress that the raft made had to be in the direction of salvation.

He had to take account of the supplies they had left. To make it, they would have to pool every man's possessions. There was no other way.

David would ensure that the raft was sound. He'd have to make repairs, if that's what it took. Without their floating craft, they would not live long. David shuddered. He had barely checked it after the storm, and he had not done so since.

"Hold on to my feet," he told Toro, whose face was sullen when he uncovered it. "I'm going to check the bottom of the raft."

"What's the use?" Toro gave him a dismissive shrug.

David looked at the despondent man with little patience. "I'm not giving up. Are you?"

Toro curled his upper lip and snorted like a child whose parents have taken away his toy.

As Toro removed his straw hat, David explained his plan. "First, I'm going to take a look at the fittings of the rudder. If any bolts are gone, you'll have to hand me some wire to replace them. Then you'll hold me as I check the packing foam all around the raft."

Toro knelt and clamped his hands on David's ankles without a word. David put his trust in Toro. He had no choice. He leaned over the side.

"Move the tiller from side to side," David yelled.

Toro pressed his shoulder against David's legs to keep him from slipping. Removing one hand from David's ankle he shifted the tiller.

"Good job! It's holding up!" David's voice rose from the side.

David wriggled his upper body like a snake and inched his way slowly around the outside of the raft. Toro held on to David's ankles and followed his movements. David's head was inches from the frothy peaks. His hands explored the synthetic foam and the protective wood frame.

"Everything's in good shape!" he reported.

As he came around the prow, he leaned down once again. Here, he felt a board giving slightly to the pressure of his hand.

"Lower me a little. I have to check a board underneath."

As Toro let David's ankles slide down a few inches, David took a deep breath and lowered his head into the water. The salt stung his eyes, but he adjusted to it immediately. David followed the length of the board with his hand and examined its condition. He was relieved there was little damage and the board would hold up.

Suddenly, a flashing movement ignited his senses. A gray form rose from the depths with the speed of lightning. David's arms thrashed in the water and his mouth opened in terror. He jerked his head out over the waves as swiftly as the bubbles that had escaped his mouth.

"Pull me up!" he managed to scream while gasping for air.

David doubled up his body like a caterpillar trying to lift himself far from the surface. Toro pulled with all his strength, gripping clothes and flesh, hand over hand, until David landed safely back on the bottom of the raft.

"You look like you saw a ghost!" Toro laughed, kneeling and catching his breath over David's trembling body. He had regained his dry sense of humor.

David's chest rose and fell as he drew great gulps of air. "What I saw was the devil himself!"

The two laughed heartily, releasing the discouragement in their hearts.

Chapter
9

Toro had had two opportunities to get rid of David, yet both times Toro had worked hard to save him. He had paddled furiously to rescue the stranded David from the abandoned raft. Now, he had pulled David back on board when a shark was about to attack. And Toro's attempt to secure Miguel to the raft made David squirm with guilt. David's feelings about Toro were changing. It had not happened suddenly. A gradual sense of fellowship had been replacing his disgust for the rafter. David shared defeat and laughter with him, where before only hate had driven their exchanges.

The men leaned back against the boards and faced each other, still catching their breath. Although they had laughed nervously, the ordeal with the shark had shaken them both.

"I might never see my sister again, you realize," Toro said with a bit of sadness. "We should be prepared for whatever comes."

"What's coming?" Luis asked, his eyes wide open with apprehension. He had watched the men scramble and laugh.

Toro and David exchanged glances and slowly shook their heads. Luis had to be dealt with gently lately, like one would treat a child.

"Nothing, Luis," David answered softly. "If something was coming, you'd be the first to see it. You're our official look-out."

Luis turned obediently and scanned the horizon.

"My sister took me in after our mother died," Toro continued. His voice was lifeless. "I've lived with her and her two children for the last few years. We did what we could to eat, but it's been hard. There's no food or hope in this Cuba of ours. You depend totally on the government and it doesn't do much for you. I am sick of it!"

"Did you tell her you were 'jumping off?'" David asked, noticing the man had been deeply troubled since they'd been forsaken by the ship. Toro had never spoken about his family. Had Toro opened up to him earlier on the trip, David might not have heard him out. Now, David listened with interest.

"No, I figured she was better off not knowing my business, in case she's taken in for questioning. If I make it to Miami, I will call her." Toro shrugged halfheartedly. "I never explained to my sister how I got the extra food that I brought home. Whenever I had good luck, her eyes glowed with relief and we ate well . That's all that mattered." Toro rubbed his temples and his eyes shut tightly for a moment. "I was driven to do things that would make my mother roll in her grave."

David knew that many people broke the unjust laws so they could make a living. He wondered to what extent Toro had gone. But he didn't ask. He nodded with sympathy.

"A man can't live that way forever. I wanted to sleep without guilt and fear. I wanted to know that my work would pay off, that I would be able to eat each day."

"That's why we left too," David agreed. "My father was looking for a better life for us."

Toro's lips compressed with regret. His dark eyes had a far away look. "At least your girl didn't turn on you!"

"You left a girl behind? What happened? Did she run off with someone else?" David asked teasingly, as Toro had done to him whenever the subject of Elena had come up.

"None of your business!" Toro shouted and clammed up. He regretted letting it slip out. It was a raw sore in his heart.

David guessed Toro had been deeply hurt and could not talk about his girl. David held back a smile. He had discovered a weak spot in Toro's side.

Through the anger Toro had at first inspired in him, David had assumed that his heart was evil. Now, he doubted that Toro's crass impulsive ways were set off by malice. His rude bossiness might have grown out of an unfair cut of his share in life. Maybe David had read Toro wrong.

"It's all over! We're doomed!" Luis screamed in panic suddenly, startling David and Toro. "It was the only way we'd make it! There's no hope now!"

"What's wrong, Luis?" David asked with concern.

"It's gone! I put my trust in St. Anthony and the statue is gone!" Luis was close to tears.

"The string probably wore out and it fell off," David tried to assure him, though he feared something more sinister had happened.

Toro shook his head, a weak smile returning to his face. Luis put such faith in superstition!

"I don't think so," Luis said convinced. He whispered in awe, "It was the devil! I heard you say it. You saw him under the raft! He took St. Anthony!"

Toro and David glanced at each other, then erupted into laughter.

Luis looked at them puzzled. "Have you lost your minds? You shouldn't laugh at the devil!"

His words fed the men's laughter. But David tried to control his amusement and think of a way to calm the man. If they told Luis the truth, he was likely to work himself into a fit of fright over the returning shark.

"The devil doesn't live in the ocean," Toro said patiently, but he couldn't help the little smile that flashed over his lips.

Luis seemed satisfied with Toro's logic. But he was affected by the loss of his plastic guardian. Luis resumed his lookout post, his body trembling and his face furrowed with lines of fear. He examined the whitecaps for signs of fins. Then he inspected the dark green water close to the raft. There, with half its body obscured by the shadow of the raft, the streamlined beast glided silently.

"It's under us! The devil! ¡*El diablo*!" Luis screamed, stuttering with dread.

Sitting by his father's side, David shook his head disappointed. Luis had discovered the shark and now would cower in fright for hours.

"The shark won't hurt us. We're safe on the raft." David spoke softly, as he remembered his father doing when David was a child in need of support.

"We've got to fight him! We can't let him get away with this!"

"Get away with what?" Toro asked in disbelief. Luis was so confused, he was really losing it.

"He took St. Anthony! Now he wants to knock us into the water!"

"Luis! Come to your senses!" David begged fruitlessly. "Sharks can't think like we can! He has no plans to get us!"

Luis continued his frantic argument, his eyes never leaving the water. "He's the devil himself! He took our savior! He took our only help! He won't give up until he gets us! I'll show him!"

Surprising Toro and David with his agility, Luis took an oar and shoved the flat end into the water. The impact sent a slap of salt water across Luis' face. Startled, he screamed, "I'll get you for that! You'll be sorry when I'm finished with you!"

"Stop that!" David ordered.

"Put the oar down!" Toro yelled.

Luis slid the long weapon at an angle under the raft and lunged at the unseen enemy. The activity sent the curious shark back up to investigate. Suddenly, within arm's length, three dull gray forms swirled just below the choppy surface.

"¡*Diablos*! Devils! Give me back my St. Anthony! I'll knock all of you senseless!" Luis ranted. He plunged his wooden weapon into the green waters. He lunged at the restless fish and they bolted soundlessly past the oar. "I'll teach you not to mess with me! I'll show you who's the boss!"

"Stop that, Luis!" David shouted again, watching the sharks with apprehension. "You're just driving them wild!"

Luis didn't hear. Feverishly, he concentrated on fighting the threatening enemy. He sank the oar into the depths as though it were a harpoon, never causing the animals the intended harm.

"Quit it!" David yelled. He grabbed Luis' arm and attempted to restrain him. Luis shook him off.

David, losing his balance on the rocking craft, kneeled down by his side.

"You're going to get us killed!" Toro roared.

"No! I'm going to get St. Anthony back! He's going to take us to land!"

Luis was driven to a fury. His marine opponents were frenzied. Soundlessly, their open jaws displayed multiple rows of sharp teeth. Drawing back his lips tightly, Luis exposed his clenched teeth. Labored grunts sounded in his throat. Suddenly, Luis plunged the useless weapon deeply into the water once more. His hands, gripping the oar firmly, followed the momentum of his downward stroke into the water. As a shark swiftly veered and approached the splashing wrists, Luis panicked. Releasing the oar, he raised his hands quickly out of the predator's reach.

"*¡Diablo!* You took St. Anthony but you won't get me!" he swore at the beast.

"What have you done?!" David shouted.

Toro scrambled to Luis' side. "*¡Idiota!* Get out of my way!"

Luis trembled. Drops of sweat dripped from his weather-beaten face. His eyes intently followed the darting fish.

The oar bobbed and dipped, its submerged end raising up slowly. Toro leaned over the water, but the oar slipped beyond his grasp.

"Try to get it back with this one!" David said, handing him the handle of the other oar.

Stretching, Toro reached for the drifting red oar with his oar, uselessly slapping the surface with the tip. The distance to it now was wider than the length of his oar. Toro made short desperate sweeps, attempting to bring the raft closer to the drifting paddle.

"It's no use. It's gone," David said, resigned to this new loss.

Toro knew he was right. He watched the red oar bob and drift further from them, three gray fins breaking the water around it from time to time. He was angry at Luis, but Luis didn't seem aware of his senseless act. His intense eyes kept watch on the living menace. His arms flailed.

"Come back here! Bring back my St. Anthony!" Luis leaned over the side, as if reaching for the disappearing sharks.

"Get back on the raft!" David shouted at him. "You're going to fall into the water!" David needed something to replace the agitated man's loss. He was endangering them and wasting their precious energy.

David worked his way to his father's side and reached into the unconscious man's pocket. Though he doubted Miguel could hear, he whispered respectfully, "Papi, I have to borrow the statue of Our Lady of Charity. Luis needs it more than you do now." Turning to the back of the raft, he grabbed one of Luis' hands and put the statue in it. "She rescued three shipwrecked sailors from the ocean. See the little men at her feet?"

Luis stared enraptured at the figure in his hand. David pointed to the tiny head of each ceramic sailor and named it, "Toro, David and Luis. She'll save us, like she saved these three many years ago." David wasn't sure he believed his own words, but he was satisfied that Luis did. Luis cradled the statue in his hands and peacefully closed his eyes to pray.

"It might as well be the devil himself who comes to get us!" Toro told David bitterly. "We're just wasting away bit by bit! Sharks are circling us like waiting buzzards."

David would not let the loss of the oar bring him down. "We have to keep our goal clear in our minds. We're heading for Florida. That's what my father would say right now, if he could." David glanced at Miguel.

Toro shrugged, dismissing David's words with a jerk of his head.

David knew their situation was critical. They were weak and in need of water and rest. To survive as long as possible, they would have to pool the group's supplies and ration what was left. Although he and Toro had crossed a barrier in their new friendship, David wondered how Toro would react to pooling and sharing their meager supplies.

"If we're going to make it, we're going to have to share what we have left." David glanced at his companions. Luis guarded the waters with fervor. Toro held David's gaze without comment. He knew David's words were meant for him.

"There's a gallon of water from the supplies my father and I brought, Luis' half gallon and a little in the canteen we found." David watched Toro, expecting an inventory of his water.

Toro took his time. They were desperate. He had given up on any notion they'd be rescued at sea. Their only hope was to make it to land. And who was to say how long that would take? He couldn't sit and watch while his companions wasted away. Toro feared losing control of his supplies, but he knew sharing was the only decent choice. He loosened the rope that secured the opening of his duffel bag.

"Take it all!" he shouted. "I have a jug of water and four crackers in my bag. Here's the bag of crackers," he said, placing it on the space between them.

David was relieved. Toro was cooperating. "There are six crackers left in my tin." David placed the tin at their feet, like poker players raising stakes.

Toro reached down to the bottom of his canvas duffel. But, as he grabbed the handle of the jug and lifted it, his face paled. "There's nothing in it! It's empty!"

Toro's peeling hand shook as he took out the jug and inspected it in the sunlight.

"There's a crack on the side. It must have happened during the storm. Everything took a rough beating," David said, feeling sorry for the man. Then, realizing the significance of the loss for the group, he shuddered.

"*¡Mal rayo lo parta!*" Toro cursed loudly, wishing a lightning strike upon the broken jug. Deep wrinkles of frustration etched his brow. His cracked lips pressed together, turning them white as the blood retreated from them.

He would have been more sparing in his swigs from the previous jug, had he known it to be his last. Toro had counted on this jug. It meant the difference between survival and death. Without water a man was doomed!

Toro lifted the empty plastic bottle and with a painful, guttural cry slammed it upon a wood beam. "Arrrg!"

Luis jumped in his seat, bewildered.

"There's nothing to be done about it," David said with empathy, trying to take away some of the pain. He knew the horror of finding one's supply of water gone. "We'll just have to ration what we have very carefully."

Toro felt he lived now at David's mercy and whim. This boy, in whom he had placed little faith, controlled his destiny. "This is what it's come to," he said despondently. "It's ironic. I left Cuba so that I wouldn't have to depend on anyone. Now, I have to rely on you to make it."

David brushed off his bitterness with a shrug. "We're all in this together. From the moment we jumped off, we put our lives in each others' hands."

Toro said no more, but his face reflected his inner anguish. David left him to his thoughts. He knew that the man, having gruffly demanded his seat on the raft, was now dependent on the group. Toro had a proud streak in him. He was probably having a difficult time coming to terms with the loss of his independence.

The rolling whitecaps lapped against the side. The sail, bulging with the force of the breeze, offered the only sign of hope.

After a while, Toro broke his silence. "Look David, it's just a matter of time." Toro slipped down to the bottom of the raft, his legs sprawled, his head propped up on a board. "We'll live only as long as the water lasts. It's as simple as that."

"Well then," David replied, "while it lasts, I'm not giving up. I'll work to hold our course and keep the raft afloat." He knew how grim their future was. He couldn't allow Toro to pull him down with him.

"You do what you think you must." Toro gave a slight shrug. "Since you're such a wishful thinker, maybe you can call my sister and tell her how I reached my end."

Toro was losing the will to fight. David smiled. He refused to take Toro seriously.

"It's been bugging me for a while," Toro said wearily. "Since we found the abandoned raft, the thought won't leave my mind. No one will ever know who those people were. No one can grieve for them. The truth is..." Toro captured David's eyes with his. He paused. Then, his painful words dragged out the turmoil in his soul. "I don't want to die the way they did, like nameless souls!"

The roots of David's hairs quivered, like a million ants scouring his skin. The thought had crossed his mind also. It had given him an unworldly sense of discomfort. But he attended to Toro's distress to relieve his own in the process. Playing along with him, David tilted a brow and squinted an eye. "I know who you are."

A tremor traveled down Toro's spine, agitating his composure. If David knew the truth about his identity, would he have the good will to share his water?

David continued. "When I get to Miami, I'll let everyone know that the 'Great Toro' sailed with us. It will be in all the Spanish newspapers in Miami. They'll announce it on all the radio stations, I'll make sure of that. In Cuba, everyone will tune in to hear about the courageous end of Toro."

David's smile was broad and innocent. Toro relaxed. David didn't know about his involvement with Pepe in the butchering of the cow.

"Your sister in Cuba will hear about it. Even your girl will be proud. She'll regret having left you."

"Cut it out!" Toro said annoyed that David had mentioned his girl again. He didn't need unpleasant reminders now.

David chuckled. Toro had teased him on the same subject before, but now David had the upper hand.

Toro was sure his end was coming soon. He would have to take a chance, even if David turned on him. He couldn't bear dying as an unknown. It was too harsh and humiliating an end.

"Look, my sister doesn't know me as Toro. This is a nickname I had on the streets. When I got into trouble, I stopped giving people my real name."

"So, what's the name I should give to the newspapers and radio?" David's mouth curled into a grin.

Toro took a breath and, watching David for a sign of recognition on his face, said, "Tomás Pico. That's my real name."

"Tomás Pico," David said nodding. He repeated the name in his head. Tomás Pico. It seemed so familiar. He was sure he had heard it before.

Noting no change in David and convinced he would not make it, Toro urged him. "Remember my name so you can write to my sister after you push my limp body into the ocean. Her address is in my duffel bag."

Recognition flashed through David's mind like a burst of gunpowder. He knew who Tomás Pico was! It seemed like an eternity since they'd left home, but the foggy curtain of memory now parted. Tomás Pico had gone to the country to butcher the cow with Pepe. He had abandoned his friend in the pasture. Because of Tomás Pico, David had been jailed!

"You are the one who left Pepe behind! That was you. Wasn't it?" David shouted angrily.

Toro sat up and looked at him with distrust. "I went to the country with Pepe. We butchered a cow together..."

"But you didn't leave together, did you?" David cut him off sarcastically.

Toro leaned back against the framing board, but a defensive scowl lingered on his face. "So? I couldn't help it if he got caught! How could I fight against armed guards?"

David was furious. He pounced on Toro and grabbed him by the shirt collar. "Because of you I lost my bicycle and got thrown in jail! And you left Pepe stranded in the field!"

Toro raised his arms and waved his hands defensively. "I wasn't in the pasture when the police arrived. I had already left with a bundle of beef."

"You admit you took the beef?" David's mouth gaped open. He tightened his grip on Toro's shirt and shook him. "You're a coward and a dirty thief! To steal from our unscrupulous government is honorable. To steal from a friend makes you a dirty thief!"

Toro took a deep breath and snorted. "I wasn't stealing from Pepe! I would never stoop that low! I gave Pepe's share of the meat to his mother."

David squinted his green eyes with resentment. He wouldn't listen to Toro's lame excuses. "I wanted to wring Tomás Pico's neck when I was released from jail! I spent three days in a hot stinking cell because of you! If my father and I had known who you were, you'd never have set foot on this raft!" David's finger poked Toro's chest directly over the heart.

Toro's voice quavered. David couldn't tell if it was from fear or righteousness. "I didn't know whose bicycle it was! I didn't leave it behind to get you in trouble."

"But that's how it turned out! State Security thought I had been Pepe's partner when they found my bicycle."

"When I found out they'd taken in the owner of the bicycle, I figured they wouldn't keep you for long. You weren't anywhere near the pasture that night."

"I suppose you were going to assure them of that?" David cocked his head, his eyes piercing Toro to the core. "I bet you felt pretty good that the heat was off your behind. It was me they were investigating!"

Toro remembered those weeks when he feared his name would be linked to the crime. All along, State Security had been investigating David. Toro had difficulty holding back the guilty smile that flashed across his face. "That doesn't mean I wasn't worried they'd find me!"

"Scum!" David's tight fist sprung back, set to strike. He wanted to smash Toro's insolent face. For endless moments, the tense fist wavered, the green eyes burned into Toro's brown eyes.

But something inside David held him back. The intimacy that the close quarters had forced on them had revealed another side of Toro's nature. Punching him for revenge, now that the man was down, suddenly became repulsive. David released his grip on the collar and Toro dropped back against the side beams.

"I'm telling you, Pepe and I had a plan," Toro continued in his own defense, fanning his head with the wide-brimmed peasant hat. It was important that David knew he had acted fairly toward his friend. "I was to hide the meat and later, we would return to the hiding place with the truck. I was taking a bundle of meat to our hiding place when the police arrived. I wish I'd had a way to save Pepe! I could see him through the bushes where I hid. He was surprised in the bare pasture, with nothing around him but the cow's remains and the bicycle. He looked like a hobbled goat about to be sacrificed."

"All because of you! Pepe and I were the sacrifice!"

"Think what you want!" Toro shouted, straightening up and arranging his wrinkled shirt. His round eyes bulged with anger at David's unjust accusations. "All I could do was save my hide. I took off through the woods. I did what Pepe would have done if it had been his job to hide the meat. He chose to do the butchering!"

David shook his head. "Pepe can't defend himself from the lies you spread to cover up your cowardice!"

"That's it! I'm not going to argue with you anymore! I was there. I know what I did and I can live with myself." His conscience was clear. He wasn't going to lower himself to David anymore. He felt as if he was begging for his life. "If you want to keep your precious water from me, it's just as well. My final days won't drag out like yours will!"

Toro's words hit David like a cold splash. "Just because you betray your friends, don't assume I can turn my back on my enemies," David answered proudly.

Chapter

10

Exhaustion had forced David into a quiet slumber on their fifth night at sea. When the first rays of morning colored the eastern horizon, David adjusted the vessel's course and looked after Miguel. Hours had passed since anyone had spoken. In light of their dire situation, his resentment of Toro had mellowed. David's eyes met Toro's as he handed out rations to each man: a stale cracker and a carefully measured drink of water. The usual fire in the round dark eyes was gone. David thought Toro was losing all hope of survival.

"I'm going for help!" Luis suddenly announced.

Toro and Luis stared at the man. The statue of the Lady of Charity trembled in his hands. His brown features were gaunt. His skinny frame hunched over from loss of weight and exhaustion.

"Where are you going?" David asked, puzzled. The man had been tittering between reality and a dream world for days.

"I'm going to swim to the island." Luis' face reflected a determination that raised the men's attention.

"What island?" Toro and David shouted together. They looked to the west and then all around them. No land was to be seen.

"Where's the island?" David asked breathlessly, his heart pounding.

"Right there," Luis said, pointing. "It's covered with grass."

David's hands drew into tight fists. If the man's mind wasn't so far gone, he'd break his nose! "That's just a bed of seaweed!"

"I can't believe you got us all excited for this!" Toro turned away from Luis angrily.

David followed the slim man's actions warily. Luis set down the statue with great care. He seemed to mumble words of respect to it. Then, deliberately, he unbuttoned his shirt and folded it. He slipped his feet out of his canvas shoes, lining them up side by side. Without any indication that he had heard them, Luis stood up on the rowing seat and told the others, "I'll be right back."

David's jaw fell open. Before he could speak, Luis raised his hands over his head, bent his knees and sprang expertly into the water.

"What are you doing? Are you crazy?" David shouted, his heart racing. His words were of no use, Luis' sleek form glided away just below the surface.

Toro and David watched on the verge of panic.

"He's really lost it!" Toro yelled.

Luis surfaced and began to swim toward the floating bed of gulfweed.

"Get back here!" David shouted, a great fear overtaking his senses.

Turning his head and waving casually at his companions, Luis hollered, "I'll be back with help! Wait for me!"

David shook his head in frustration. "How can he expect we'll stop and wait for him?"

"There is no island! Come back to the raft!" Toro stood up angrily. He grabbed a rope and knotted it. "If I have to come after you, I'll kill you!"

Despite his anxiety, David looked up at Toro and smiled at the absurdity of his threat. "You'd save him just to kill him?"

"I'm so mad at him right now, I could!" He slipped the loop of rope over his head and slid it down to his waist. "Hold the end!" he told David without explanation.

"What do you think you're doing?" David was aghast. His brows arched, startled.

"Just pull when I tell you," Toro demanded. He had no time to waste.

Luis moved through the water with regular strokes, amazing the others with his reserve of energy. He was cutting the distance to the flotsam without regard to the dreaded predators of the sea.

"I can't have both of you in the water!" David attempted a command. But apprehension marked his words as he struggled to bring Toro back to his senses.

"Just pray we make it back!" With little thought for his personal safety, Toro threw his straw hat aside and dived off the stern into the dark green water.

The coolness shocked his burning skin. Salt stung his eyes. He glided under the surface until the power of the dive was spent. His head, covered with clumped matted hair, broke the surface.

David's eyes followed every movement, never blinking for fear of missing any of the dangerous activity.

Toro's arm rose above the surface, and he began a rhythmic crawl toward the enormous bed of sargassum. His face came out of the water every few strokes, for a breath of air and to keep an eye on the receding Luis.

David was surprised at Toro's ability to keep up the effort. Luis seemed to be slowing down. His movements were not as smooth as before. Since the tragic storm, they had been spared from rough seas. David was thankful that only gentle rolls played on the surface this morning.

"Wait for me! You crazed fool!" Toro yelled at Luis.

His command had the intended result. Luis turned and waited, treading water at the edge of the weeds. "We're almost there! Hurry up!"

Toro was by his side in two powerful strokes. He wrapped his arm around Luis' thin waist and turned back to the raft.

"Pull on the rope!"

David went to work. Looking for a pulley, he coiled the rope around the stake that had served as an oarlock. Despite this precaution, the rough rope scratched his palms as he took all the slack from it. The effort of pulling the weight of both bodies through the water made his muscles tense and sore.

"No, no! You're taking us the wrong way!" Luis shouted and fought to free himself from the protective embrace. "The island's over there!"

Luis' feet kicked and treaded underwater, striking Toro's thighs painfully. His frantic efforts canceled Toro's one-handed strokes in the opposite direction.

"¡*Ya basta*! Enough! You're going back with me!" Toro shouted, taking in an unexpected gulp of salt water. He gasped and coughed, never letting go of his grip on the anxious man's waist.

"Let go of me!" Luis screamed as he grappled with his rescuer. Luis' hands landed on Toro's shoulders and pushed.

"You're forcing me to do this," Toro warned. He had no choice. He wouldn't let the man take them both to their death. He brought his free hand up, clenched it into a tight fist and struck Luis in the face. Stunned, Luis gave up the struggle.

"Pull us back!" Toro shouted, and immediately felt the rope tighten and slip up to his armpits. He gripped Luis securely under the arms and pumped the water briskly with his legs. His free arm firmly slashed the water. The exertion made his heart beat furiously.

David's hands burned. He circled his backside with the rope and leaned back on it. The small raft swiveled with the pull of his effort and the resistance of the weight. He grunted loudly.

The men were now at the side of the vessel. David released the rope and reached into the water. Grabbing Luis under the arms, David lifted as the skinny, confused man pulled himself back on board. Reaching back over the side, David gripped the rope that circled Toro's middle.

"On the count of three, pull up on the wood beam," he told the gasping man.

David counted, and the two men pooled their energies as one. But the effort wasn't enough. Toro slipped back down into the lapping green water. In between labored breaths, David teased him, "You're too heavy."

On the second try, with David leaning back to balance the tilting raft as he pulled on Toro's rope, they made it.

Toro dropped to the bottom of the raft, exhausted. His chest expanded with each deep breath.

"Thanks," he said to David, catching his gaze with tired eyes.

When their lungs were satisfied back to a normal breathing rhythm, Toro slipped the rope from around his chest. "I'm going to make sure you don't pull another stunt like this one again!" he said to Luis, who sat at the stern, still dripping. "You see this loop?" Toro asked, slipping it over the dark man's head.

David shot up, fearing he'd use it as a noose. "You're not going to carry out your threat!"

"I should tighten it around his neck," Toro said smoothly. Then, winking an eye at David, he rolled the circle of rope down to Luis' middle. "But this is a belt to hold up his pants."

With instant understanding of his intentions, David grabbed the end of the rope and tied it firmly to a beam. "This will keep your pants from falling off!"

David and Toro exchanged a conspiratorial glance. Then they settled back tiredly.

"I can't believe you dived into the water after Luis," David said.

"He's so lost," Toro said, glancing at Luis, who quietly dried off in the sun. "I couldn't bear to see him die in such confusion."

"Weren't you scared to drown?" David asked, amazed. "Weren't you afraid of the sharks?"

Toro's brows shot up. "I forgot about them." He smiled and shrugged. "You can't give those things much thought in a crisis like that. You simply do what's right."

David had come to admire Toro. He'd found that Toro could be unselfish and brave. In spite of Toro's low opinion of Luis, he had put the man's life above his own.

Toro spoke. "I wasn't sure if you'd leave me to drown and sink."

"What makes you think I'd do that?" David shot back. How could Toro would think that low of him?

"You were so angry with me yesterday when I told you who I was…"

David shrugged and looked away. Although he had resented Toro for being the cause of his incarceration, his anger for the man was no longer driving him. He'd had reason to be angry before. But that was while on dry land, at a time when their human struggles were measured in standard scales. In the confined world of the raft, at the mercy of the harsh elements, one couldn't judge a person the same way. On the ocean, there was no time for pretensions; a wrong choice meant disaster. The tests they had endured drew out their true selves. And David had grown to respect what he had seen in Toro.

"I can't blame you. Even Mirta wouldn't believe that it wasn't my fault." Toro nodded with resignation.

David's face brightened, guessing Toro had dodged questions about girlfriends because of this. "Is Mirta your *novia*?"

Toro made a face of disgust. "That's what I thought. It turned out she had turned sweet on Pepe. She insisted I had run out on him. I'm sure she's been spreading rumors about me abandoning Pepe in the field."

Perhaps Toro wasn't lying about what happened. State Security would have persuaded Pepe to name his partner in the butchering. They had ways to make people talk. David shuddered. Why would Pepe remain silent if he had been angry at Toro? Toro carried a personal identification card, as did everyone else in Cuba, and was licensed to drive a truck. State Security certainly knew where to find him if his name had been associated with the crime.

"I'm sorry your girlfriend turned on you," David said, feeling badly for his new-found friend. "I've kept my sanity thinking about Elena. It's the only thing that brings me joy on this endless trip."

Toro smiled and nodded. "She's a pretty girl. You're lucky."

"Do you want to see her picture again?" David didn't wait for an answer. He fished the plastic envelope from his shirt and, taking a quick appraising glance, handed it to Toro.

Toro looked into David's green eyes. There was wisdom behind the friendly open smile on David's face. Toro wondered why he had not noticed it before. Maybe David had grown through their ordeal at sea.

Their peaceful chat was broken suddenly. "Look at that skull! It's floating in the water!" Luis yelled.

"A skull can't float in the water!" Toro said, impatient at the man's confused visions.

"I'm telling you I saw it over there, on the grass! It's gone now." Luis pointed excitedly, then cowered. "I'll bet it's the devil himself, coming back for us!"

Toro shook his head, making the shadow of his wide brimmed hat swivel on his shoulders. "He's got me all worked up with his visions of the devil and savior saints," he confided to David. "I don't know what I saw last night, but I was sure it was the lights of hell!"

Although a smile danced on David's lips, an ominous chill sprinted through him. "You too? Maybe you have reason to worry and someone's giving you a glimpse of hell," David teased.

"It was eerie," Toro said, leaning forward to confide. "The sky glowed brightly, as if an intense heat burned at its base. The air seemed dense and thick and an orange glare shined in the direction the raft was pointing."

David listened with interest. "The glow came from the northwest?"

"Why do you ask? Is that where hell is?" Toro's joking smile showed off the gap in his teeth.

David's eyes opened wide and his brows rose. "Why didn't you wake me?"

"Wake you? And risk having you shove me off the raft?" Toro chuckled. He wondered why David acted as though he had missed out on something important.

David grabbed the man's arms, kneeling at his feet with uncontrollable joy. "What you saw was the lights of Miami! Rafters say they've seen the orange glow in the sky! We're not far away! We're almost there!" David shook Toro's arms, amazed at the news.

David's excitement was contagious. Toro's round eyes gleamed with hope. Luis smiled broadly.

David crawled to his father's side and lifted the cap from his face. "Papi! We're close to Miami! We'll get everything you need! Just have patience, Papi!" David thought he detected a slight movement of his father's head. He took it as an indication that Miguel had heard him.

"There's the skull again!" Luis said with hushed apprehension.

"It's a turtle!" Toro announced, surprised. He twisted around in his seat and leaned over the side for a better look.

The large turtle swam in the sargassum bed, heedless of the strange craft. Its golden flippers and head were covered with copper plates. The shoulder of its brown shell emerged from the surface for a moment, as the animal stretched its neck to pluck a morsel from the weeds. David could see how the bony head with its glassy dark eyes could resemble a floating skull.

"It's swimming this way!" David's green eyes shone with enthusiasm.

Toro turned to David. "Quick, grab the oar and push the turtle towards me when it swims by. We'll catch it and eat it!"

David swung into action, energized by the prospect of filling his stomach again. "Get your knife! Stab him in the neck when you grab it!"

"Great idea!" Toro pulled the knife from the belt of his pants. He bit down on the blade to free up his hands, as he'd seen done in a Tarzan movie long ago. He grinned and his eyebrows shot up with anticipation.

Spotting the unusual craft, the curious logger-head dove under. Paddling swiftly with its long front flippers, it resurfaced at the raft's side, snorting a spray of water and air.

The two young men sprang into action, working together as a practiced team. David swung the red oar over Toro's kneeling frame. He reached past the turtle's carapace and, calling on all his strength, David drove the animal against the wood beams of the raft. The large loggerhead was trapped. Its flippers flailed. Toro reached down and grabbed the hard edges of the animal's shell.

"Pull it up!" David yelled. He huffed and his muscles strained as he held the oar in place.

Toro jerked up on the cornered reptile with all his might. But the creature's shell barely raised up above the surface. Its urgent flapping drenched its adversaries with salt water. Toro snorted to drive the stinging spray out of his nose.

David's arms trembled from the violent effort. "Lift it up! I can't hold it in place much longer!"

Luis leaned over the side, as far as his binding rope would extend, to take part in the conflict. He seized a slippery back flipper, which flapped with unexpected vigor. Luis' arms bounced up and down with the energetic struggles of the turtle.

Toro's nose flared as his lungs took in a big reserve of air. The muscles of his arms swelled. His teeth clenched tightly on the warm metal of the knife blade. He lifted the struggling weight half-way up, water running off the protective covering of the animal. But Toro's effort was no match for the large heavy turtle.

"Stab it! Stick the knife into his neck!" David screamed anxiously.

Toro sputtered, unable to speak with the metal blade held in his teeth. He feared that if he reached for the knife, he wouldn't be able to hold onto the flapping animal with only one hand. But he had to try. He grabbed the butt of the knife with his right hand and his left hand ached, keeping a grip on the sharp edge of the carapace.

"Do it! I can't hold on anymore!"

"Aaaah!" Toro plunged the knife with primeval satisfaction.

The sharp blade entered the waters and the fist gripping the handle tightly followed, breaking the surface with a splash. The knife found no resistance! With powerful strokes of its muscular front flippers, the turtle freed itself from confinement and submerged.

Toro's sudden burst of laughter ripped through the shock of the crew. His throbbing arms dangled loosely over the side and his head faced the empty green waters.

His deep hoarse laughter was catching. David threw his head back and joined him, his rich sound a mixture of release and frustration. He plopped down to the bottom of the raft, dropping the heavy oar with a loud noise as it hit the boards.

Toro turned around to face him and extended a hand. He was exhausted, but his laughter was full of life. "That was a good job, partner!"

David gripped the friendly hand. "The turtle's still the winner."

"He must have weighed three hundred pounds!"

"And we thought we would bring him in!" David's voice rode on the waves of his laughter.

Luis watched them with amusement, truly not comprehending the bizarre reaction of the two men.

"That turtle took off like a nuclear submarine! It must be five miles away, hiding in the corals!" Toro couldn't go on, he was shaking with another fit of laughter.

"The water was so clear..." David paused, sobering up as he recognized the signs.

Toro interrupted a chuckle, his thoughts traveling with the speed of a rocket. He finished David's sentence, "...I could see the bottom!"

David's hands trembled, when he brought them to his brow to shadow his eyes. Toro scanned the horizon with him. "Can you see anything?" Toro asked, an unusual note of anticipation in his voice.

The rumble of emotion that surged in David exploded. "There! Look over there! Can you see the dark line?"

"¡*Tierra*! ¡*Tierra*! I see land!" Toro burst out.

"Over there, too! And there!" David pointed to parts of a long dark line along the western horizon. His voice bubbled with excitement.

Toro removed his hat, placing it over his chest. His dark eyes bulged in amazement.

Luis stood up. His face was radiant. He clutched the statue of the Lady of Charity and repeated over and over, "*Ya llegamos*. We've arrived."

Toro put his arm around the simple, thin man. "*Sí, mi amigo. Ya llegamos*."

※※※※※※

David fought to control the swell of emotion that filled him. As he took the receiver from Gabriel, his hand trembled.

"Mami?" He paused, afraid his voice would crack.

"¡*Mi hijo*!" Rosa responded upon hearing her beloved son's voice. A sob of relief overtook her.

"We landed in the Florida Keys!" Happiness flowed from his voice. "Papi is weak, but the doctors say he's going to be fine."

"I am so glad! I finally will be able to sleep!" She had no concern for any snoopers overhearing her open conversation. Her most fervent prayers had been answered. "Are you all right?"

"Just sunburned, that's all. Luis had a difficult time of it. But now, I'm sure he'll recover."

Her son's voice seemed to be an octave lower since she'd last spoken to him. "Diana and Elena are standing by my side. So is tío Roberto. We've all been praying for you!"

"Tell them I will write as soon as I can. And Mami, I need you to find my friend's sister. His name is Tomás Pico. Tell her he made it to freedom!" After giving Rosa Toro's sister's address, he continued.

"Gabriel says I can enroll in school and still have a job on the weekends. Papi and I are going to save our money and get you out. We won't forget you." David's voice had taken on a solemn tone. Then he chuckled. "But first, I'm going to send you a pair of leather shoes."